WHERE THE HEART BELONGS

WHERE THE HEART BELONGS

Sheila Spencer-Smith

CHIVERS

British Library Cataloguing in Publication Data available

This Large Print edition published by BBC Audiobooks Ltd, Bath, 2010
Published by arrangement with the author

U.K. Hardcover ISBN 978 1 408 45792 4
U.K. Softcover ISBN 978 1 408 45793 1

Copyright © Sheila Spencer-Smith, 2009

Printed and bound in Great Britain by
CPI Antony Rowe, Chippenham and Eastbourne

A RETURN TO HAPPINESS

'What do you think?' Shona said to the recumbent Toby jug she had placed on the passenger seat beside her. 'Shall we take a quick look?'

Laughing at herself, she glanced at the gold and black notice board as she drove in through the open gates. Ahead of her, its façade glinting in the sunshine, was Ferniehope Castle.

No towering keep or stone-walled turrets here, just a plain white building with a fancy stone balustrade and steps leading up to a stone porch.

She got out of the car, her eyes dazzled by the splendour of the place. The left-hand side of the building had an extra storey and the different pitch of the grey-tiled roof to this side gave the whole thing an elevation that was pleasing.

'Can I help you?'

She swung round, startled, and saw a tall man with a large rake balanced on one shoulder looking at her. His green T-shirt had a stain on the other sleeve and an aura of warmth surrounded him as if he had been engaged in heavy physical work.

'Um,' she gulped. 'Well no, not really. Sorry, I'll just go.'

1

She felt his interest in his direct gaze that seemed to take in every aspect of her jersey and brand new jeans. 'Surely not, now you've made the effort to come?' he said.

A strange sensation ran through her as she studied the floppy fairish hair falling over his forehead and a mouth that curved up into a beginning of a smile. She was only aware that he had spoken again when he looked at her as if expecting a reply.

'Oh, I'm sorry,' she stammered.

'Courses are run here, you know,' he said. 'Archery, origami, cordon bleu cookery, canoeing.'

'Well yes, I saw the board at the gate.'

'And?'

'Oh no, not for me. I'm on holiday.'

'No one has set up a course for ceramics as yet, I'm afraid. The tutor pulled out.' His eyes clouded for a moment. 'Was that the one you wanted?'

She shook her head. 'Oh no, I . . .'

'How about Navigation In Arctic Waters or Potholing For The Dumbfounded?'

She smiled, acknowledging that he was making fun of her. But she owed him that for wasting his time when he obviously had work to do. 'I'm really sorry for trespassing like this,' she said with humility.

He glanced round. 'No law of trespass here, you know. Broken any fences, knocked down a wall or two with that Honda of yours? If not you're quite safe.'

'I was looking for someone,' she said. 'I just wondered . . .'

'And you suspect she may be hiding away here?'

'No, no, of course not.' She didn't know what to make of him, standing there in his long grey shorts that emphasised the deep tan of his legs.

'Parts of the building date from the middle of the sixteenth century,' he said.

'They do?'

'But it can't boast of any dungeons as far as I know, only basements. You're welcome to have a quick look round. But you'll need to move your car first or I can't answer for its safety once Donald gets going on the motor mower.'

She could hear the hum of an engine now. 'Oh, no,' she said, even more eager to escape. 'I'm on my way somewhere else.'

He looked amused. 'So this was just a small entertaining diversion?'

He stayed where he was until she had turned her car and was moving slowly down the drive to the road. In her mirror she saw him wave his hand and then turn away.

Warmth flooded her face as she thought how well and truly she had been caught out when she had only intended to take a quick look at the place. Who was Rake Man, anyway, making her feel stupidly in the wrong?

3

'All your fault, Toby,' she said. 'I should have packed you away with the rest of my stored stuff. But you wouldn't have liked that, would you?'

Toby had no answer to that. In fact he wasn't much help at all sitting there in the passenger seat and staring straight ahead at nothing because he was far too small to see above the dashboard.

I'm going mad, talking to a jug, she thought.

She had discovered him hidden away at the back of the china cabinet when she and her cousin, Jodie, were clearing out her Harrogate apartment. She had pulled him out and stared at him in disbelief. 'A toby jug!'

Jodie had laughed. 'The expression on your face, Shona! You look as if you've seen a ghost.'

'It's the shock,' Shona said, laughing too.

'And no wonder.'

Shona sat back on her heels on the dusty floor and smoothed back loose strands of fair hair. 'Just look at his ugly face and thick handle. I can't think where he came from.'

'A dark secret.'

'An intriguing secret,' she said as she put the offending jug down on the floor. 'Can you imagine Mum ever using anything like this? And Dad never did for the rest of his life.'

'So you won't be packing it safely away when you head off into the unknown?' said Jodie, her eyes dancing.

4

'No way.' Shona wrapped the last piece of bone china and placed it in the box for Jodie to look after for her. Thank goodness they had nearly finished the packing now. The big furniture had gone to the salesroom already with only a few pieces left in position that Jodie and her family were welcome to use when they moved in.

Jodie got up and stretched. 'All done?'

Shona leapt up too and brushed the dust from the legs of her jeans. 'Come on, coffee time. We deserve a rest after all that hard work.'

Jodie seated herself at the kitchen table and picked up the toby jug she had brought in with her. 'He's attractive in a hideous sort of way,' she said at last. 'Someone loved him once or how did he get into the cabinet?'

'But pushed right to the back,' Shona reminded her.

Jodie gave the clumsy handle a pat before putting the jug down to take the cup of coffee Shona passed to her. 'Mmm, this is good.'

'Biscuit?'

'Don't tempt me.'

Shona plumped down too. 'I don't know about you, Jodie, but I'm shattered.'

'Full of energy, me. I can't wait to move in and get settled.'

'So you'll want me out of your way at once?'

'Of course not, Shona. You know that.'

Jodie looked so upset that Shona hastened

5

to reassure her. 'Only joking. Anyway, I'm anxious to get on my way. I'll be off at first light tomorrow and then the flat's all yours.'

'Going off on your own for a few weeks sounds wonderful,' said Jodie, a little wistfully.

Shona took a sip of her coffee and looked at her cousin with affection. 'You don't really think that,' she said. 'Duncan wouldn't like it if you went off somewhere on your own, now would he. What about the twins?'

'Well no,' said Jodie, a catch in her voice. 'I'd miss them horribly too. And we're going to love living here. I hope you won't regret it letting us have your lovely home until we find somewhere of our own.'

Shona smiled. 'It's great knowing it'll still be in the family.' She thought of the half-empty sitting room, unrecognisable now as the overheated and crowded place her father had loved.

'Uncle wasn't always easy to look after, was he?' said Jodie. 'Now's your chance to enjoy some freedom, Shona. Where are you planning on going?'

Shona gazed down at her coffee. 'I'll probably drive up through the Dales and head for Penrith and then up to Carlisle. I may linger there for a day or two if I can find a good B&B, visiting friends in the area, and then who knows . . . Scotland?'

'Galloway?' said Jodie, leaning forward eagerly. 'Why not? What fun to go back there again. I loved being all together on those family holidays when we were growing up, didn't you? Just think, you might run across Felix again.'

'Felix? I can't think what you mean.'

'No? Then why are you blushing?'

'For goodness sake, Jodie. That was years ago.'

'And that's what the toby jug reminds me of.'

Shona gazed at her cousin, memories she had damped down for years beginning to stir. The lovely area of south-west Scotland had seemed magical to her as she was growing up and hero-worshipping the young local boy they met each holiday. All nonsense, of course. Felix, intent on finding the right kind of mud from the estuary to fashion into rough and ugly pots had no eyes for her. She had nursed her secret unaware of her sharp-eyed young cousin drinking it all in.

'Remember Rich Aunt Aggie? We never met her, did we?' said Jodie.

'I always thought Felix made her up.'

'He could make anybody up, that boy. Remember the tramp on the island that turned out to be a stuffed sack? I had nightmares for weeks.'

'All so long ago.'

'You must go back there now,' said Jodie. 'Who knows, it could be fate bringing you together again.'

7

Fate? Hardly, Shona thought. She hadn't wondered before why the Galloway holidays had come to an abrupt end and had never asked. Strange really.

'And I'll want to hear all the details about Felix Langholme.'

'Don't hold your breath,' said Shona, laughing.

To cause a distraction she picked up the toby jug and ran her fingers over the shiny surface. Not even its glistening colours could disguise his ugliness, but already he was beginning to get to her. 'I think I'll take this little chap with me for company when I head north,' she said.

'And you'll visit Galloway again, won't you?'

'Maybe.'

'And make sure you text me when you get there. I'll be waiting to hear about Felix.'

'There'll be nothing to tell.'

'If you say so.'

The teasing expression in her cousin's eyes had finally made Shona's decision. No way would she have let on just then about her ex-boss's good friend who was in need of a personal assistant at his conference centre in Galloway, in case nothing came of it. Harley de Los, thriller writer, off to live in Boston with his new wife, no longer needed Shona's input as his researcher and had eagerly recommended her to Jack Cullen, but she wasn't too sure it was for her, although she needed the money.

She couldn't spoil that happy moment by hints of her own financial status. It had been good to see Jodie relaxed and optimistic about her future again after the worry of the enforced move of the family from their home.

Time enough to tell her about the position at Ferniehope Castle when she had decided what she was going to do about it.

*   *   *

From Dumfries she had intended taking the road all the way to Stranraer, but decided almost at the last minute to turn off north at Crocketford. Then at New Galloway she had headed south again and taken the road through Laurieston Forest to have a quick look at Ferniehope Castle while she was in the area. Now she wished she hadn't. Instead, she should have looked for the farm nearer the coast where her family had stayed years ago.

To her dismay she couldn't remember the name or exactly where it was. Not surprising really after twenty years. She had changed too from that naïve fifteen-year-old girl who imagined that a brief kiss from a rather vague and dreamy local boy meant more than just relief of not being cut off by the tide.

Now, that boy would be a thirty-eight-year-old man and secure enough to make fun of a supposed stranger. If the man with the rake she had just met was Felix Langholme, of course. And how likely was that? Allowing Jodie's romantic imaginings about herself and Felix to get to her was total nonsense.

The farmhouse where she eventually booked in for the night was set back from the road north of Newton Stewart. Her room on the first floor was large and airy with flowery curtains at the window.

Tired from the exertions of the day, she retired early after the evening meal and then lay awake, her mind full of the man who had accosted her at Ferniehope Castle. She wished how she had asked him if he were Felix. But what would his reaction have been? Total incomprehension of course. What else?

*   *   *

Sunlight slanting in through the long sash window woke Shona early next morning and she lay in bed savouring the luxury of being able to please herself in the plans she made for the day. Heady stuff, this total freedom after the last few traumatic months. Now that she was in the area she might as well do a little exploring to locate the place that Jodie was so keen for her to revisit. The simplest way to do that was to describe it to her hostess and ask her advice.

She sprang out of bed, eager now to get down to breakfast and to make her enquiries.

10

And also to book in for another night's accommodation.

'It's Leckie Shore you'll be wanting.'

'Yes,' said Shona, light dawning. 'Of course. I remember now. Can you tell me how to get there? Better still I've got a map in the car.' She ran to get it and then spread it out on the hall table for a close inspection.

She wasn't surprised that Leckie Shore wasn't marked on the map, but with help could pinpoint exactly where it was. She couldn't wait to get started. First, though, some shops in town for rolls, cheese and fruit for a picnic lunch. She had a couple of cans of lemonade in the car and would purchase more supplies of that, too.

*   *   *

The narrow twisting road she drove down to reach the shore of the estuary seemed to go on for miles. She passed a house and cottage that looked familiar and stopped the car for a moment to take a look. Yes, the very ones. Jodie would be pleased when she phoned her tonight.

The house had no sign outside advertising Bed and Breakfast as she had hoped. The cottage had a garage built to one side and a vegetable garden in the front. Other signs, too, showed that it was lived in permanently now and no longer a holiday let. Ah well, times change, she thought, and it was all a long time ago.

At last she saw the grey gleam of water ahead and reached the grassy edge of the land and the small curved beach on which they had spent so much of their time.

Out to sea half a mile away was the island they had thought of as their own with its small beach shining in the sunlight. This was it. This was where they had spent long summer days and where Felix had joined them, taking the lead in their games of exploration because he was the eldest.

The tide was in today, which was disappointing. She had imagined walking across the hard sand that divided the island from the mainland at low tide. Never mind, if she stayed here long enough the water would recede and she would be able to get across just as they did in the past.

She left the car parked in the shelter of gorse bushes and jumped down the steep bit to the beach. Someone had built a rough cairn of stones near the water's edge and she crunched over the stones and coarse sand to reach it and add a stone of her own.

Strange to think that others came here too when in her memories they had been the only ones peopling the area with their make-believe games. In her mind's eye she could see Felix striding along in his purple shorts oblivious of what people might think of his strange garb.

She went back to the car to get out a rug and her bag of provisions. Finding a suitable grassy patch in a slight hollow she settled down for a long wait, revelling in the scent of grass and seaweed in the air. A gentle ripple on the water disturbed the calmness and a few drifting clouds darkened the sun for a few moments. At once the scene looked sombre, the low scrubby trees on the island a little gloomy. Then out came the sun again.

Now the sound of engines disturbed the quietness and two vehicles came bumping along the track towards her. They parked a little distance away. One, a car like hers, disgorged its four passengers who rushed to the rear of the other, a Transit van with a roof rack of canoes. The door was yanked open and four more people jumped out.

Her peace disturbed by laughter and shouting, Shona watched as they all got themselves sorted out with buoyancy aids before lifting down the canoes. They carried them down to the water's edge and in no time at all were on the water making for the island.

Feeling envious, she watched their progress until they landed on the small beach on the other side and pulled the canoes out of the sea.

*　　*　　*

Time went by and the cairn of stones was

nearer the water now. The tide was still coming in. The rising breeze blew strands of hair into Shona's eyes. Behind her the distant mountains were disappearing into cloud. She shivered.

Raising her face to the sky she felt a drop of rain. Just as well to eat her lunch in the car in a place which was beginning to work its old magic on her. She wanted to stay here forever but the sky was grey now and the rain seemed to have set in for the afternoon.

Anxious about the canoeists, she ate slowly, gazing at the island that was now almost lost in the thickening mist. She had finished her meal by the time they appeared, laughing and talking, and made haste to pack up ready to depart. She would go, too.

She turned the key in the ignition and signalled to them to go first. With a wave the two vehicles were off and she followed them slowly along the track to the road.

Glancing at the passenger sea, she murmured, 'I wonder where they came from, Toby? Surely not Ferniehope Castle? It seemed likely, now she came to think of it. Had Rake Man mentioned canoeing courses in his list of delectable subjects? Yes, she was sure he had.

It occurred to her, suddenly, that working at Ferniehope Castle would mean she could stay in this lovely area. There was nothing to hold her in Harrogate, except Jodie of course, living in her old home that meant she was homeless unless she turned them out. Maybe one day Jodie could come up here for holidays, but that would have to wait until Duncan had got himself into employment again, of course. That day might be a long time coming.

Meanwhile, what of herself?

She had always intended taking a look at the place where Harley de Los' friend lived and if she liked it, contacting Jack Cullen as he had suggested. And she had liked Ferniehope Castle in spite of Rake Man.

Instead of roaming the area first she could apply for the post of personal assistant right now if she felt inclined.

'What do you think, Toby?' she said. 'Let's have an opinion out of you for a change.'

He said nothing, of course.

SHONA SEIZES AN OPPORTUNITY

The rain was thumping down on the roof of the car now and visibility was poor. Shona slowed down and through the onslaught saw that the vehicles ahead were signalling right on to the main road. On impulse she followed them until they turned left again after a few miles. Definitely the way to Ferniehope Castle, which couldn't be far away. Instead of turning left too, she signalled and pulled across into

15

the forecourt of a likely looking café that had appeared just at the right moment. Bessie's Kitchen was the sign above the door.

She leapt out and ran. Inside, the room was empty of customers but the atmosphere was warmly welcoming on this wet day. She sat at a solid pine table nearest the low picture window at the far end and looked out on to the dripping trees bordering the misty grey water.

'It's a bad day to be outside,' said the short cheerful-looking woman in a mauve jersey and skirt who came forward to serve her. Pushing her damp hair back from her face, Shona agreed.

'Now what can I get you?'

She ordered tea and scones and when they came found she was hungrier than she had thought and asked for a toasted cheese sandwich as well. When she had finished eating she saw that in the corner of the room was a stand of postcards. She got up to look at them. There were other cards, too, reproductions of original paintings.

'These are attractive,' she said. 'Are they all local scenes?'

'Mostly,' said the woman, walking across to join her and bringing with her a faint waft of flowery perfume. 'They run painting courses near here, you know, residential ones with excellent tutors. A lot of them get their cards made at the printing place they set up locally. The owner is an enterprising sort of man.'

'Jack Cullen?'

'You know him?'

'Not yet,' said Shona. 'But I'm thinking of applying for a job at Ferniehope Castle as his personal assistant.'

'You are?' The surprise in her voice was disconcerting.

Surely he hadn't filled the position already?

'Accommodation is provided, so I'm told, and that's important.'

'Good luck to you then. I'm Liz, by the way.'

'Not Bessie?'

'Bessie was my mother and I took over here when she died a couple of years ago.'

'A lovely place to live,' said Shona wistfully.

Liz's round face flushed with pleasure. 'Och yes. It's hard work in the season, of course, but hard work never killed anyone and I love it.'

'I can see you do. I think you're lucky. I'm Shona, Shona Renison, by the way.'

'And you're staying round here?'

'Just for a couple of nights. Near Newton Stewart.'

'A grand place.'

Liz put a card straight in the rack and then retired behind the counter again.

'They're booked up after that,' Shona said. 'I would have stayed on for a few days, but maybe I won't need to if I'm offered the job and Mr Cullen wants me to start at once. I do hope so.'

'That would be fine for you, Shona,' Liz

17

said.

She sounded so interested that Shona smiled. 'You see, my dad was almost an invalid at the end. I was so pleased to get a job I could do at home so I could be there for him. But now he's gone I've nothing to keep me in Harrogate.'

Liz nodded, her sympathy apparent in her luminous eyes. 'So you decided to get about a bit and see something of the world before deciding what you want to do next?'

Shona nodded. 'It seemed a good idea.'

'There's a single room vacant here if you're ever stuck. I take guests every now and again and I'd be glad of the company.'

'I may well take you up on that.' Shona smiled, delighted to have made a friend so soon. She liked Liz's friendly manner and the offer of accommodation here so close to Ferniehope Castle was welcome.

Rain was still falling when she left the warmth of Bessie's Kitchen and made a dash for the car. No more sightseeing today but straight back to the farm and a rest before the evening meal was served. She might even phone Ferniehope Castle and make enquiries about the job she hoped was still open to her.

*   *   *

Showered, and wearing clean shirt and jeans, Shona shook her damp hair away from her

18

face and sat down on her bed to dial the number for Ferniehope Castle. Now that she had made up her mind to act she was impatient to make it happen as soon as possible.

The dialling tone stopped and a rasping voice spoke. 'Ferniehope. May I help you?'

'Can I speak to Mr Jack Cullen, please?'

'You could if he was here.'

Shona sighed. Oh dear, another odd one. Ferniehope Castle was obviously full of them. Well, she was pretty odd herself talking to a toby jug. She should fit in well.

'I'll ring back later then, shall I?' she said.

'No need for that.' The voice sounded unfriendly. 'Miss Shona Renison?'

Surprised, Shona hesitated.

'Are you Miss Renison or not?'

'Yes, that's me,' Shona said quickly.

'You are speaking to the proprietor's secretary.'

'I was hoping to speak to Mr Jack Cullen.'

'Was it about something important?'

'I'm phoning about a job I understand has been advertised as personal assistant to him. My ex-boss suggested I contacted him.'

'Ex-boss?' The tone was definitely suspicious.

'That's right,' Shona said, struggling to keep her voice even. Why should she explain to this unfriendly person that Harley de Los, the thriller writer, for whom she had worked as his

19

researcher, had gone with his new American wife to make their home in the States? True, she could have continued to work for him long-distance, emailing her research results, but she didn't want that because his decision had provided the jolt she needed to make an important change in her life. Add to that Jodie and Duncan's housing problems and her decision was made.

'May I make an appointment to see him very soon?' she added.

'Mr Cullen went off to Edinburgh this morning.'

'Oh.' The disappointment in Shona's voice sounded acute even to her own ears.

'You may leave your number.'

Shona did so and then put the phone down, feeling as if she was being accused of pushiness and arrogance. Now that she had decided to make contact with Jack Cullen he wasn't available.

*   *   *

Next morning rippling shadows decorated the lawn and the branches of the trees swayed gently against the cloudless sky. A glorious morning but poignant too, Shona thought as she sat down at the breakfast table. Tomorrow someone else would be sitting here listening to the pleasant sound of birdsong through the slightly open window while choosing between the tantalising items on the menu.

Somehow the idea of travelling on somewhere new had lost its appeal.

But where was her sense of adventure, her pleasure in discovering new things while she had the chance? Toby would have something to say about it if she hadn't left him in the car.

Smiling at the idea, Shona ate her porridge and then, making an effort, decided on scrambled egg and mushrooms.

'Why not have some smoked salmon as well?' her landlady suggested with such a kind smile that Shona agreed and then was glad that she had because the locally smoked salmon was mouth-watering.

Ashamed of her earlier feelings, she poured more coffee and thought about where she would go today. It hadn't occurred to her yesterday to ask when Jack Cullen was expected home. This must be her first priority so that she could plan her time sensibly until it was possible to contact him. When she left here she would drive into town and buy provisions for a picnic lunch as she had done yesterday and then telephone Ferniehope Castle to enquire.

She paid the bill and left. Her mobile rang as she drove through the entrance and she pulled in to the side of the road to answer it.

'Miss Shona Renison?' The voice was deep and strangely familiar.

'Yes, that's me.'

21

'I understand you phoned about the job? I apologise for not being at Ferniehope to meet you yesterday.'

'Jack Cullen!' she gasped.

'The same.' He sounded amused.

She took a deep breath, struggling to hide her surprise that they had already met. Now what had she done showing herself up as an inquisitive moron? The wonder was that he had bothered to contact her now. 'I believe Harley de Los has spoken to you about me?'

'He did that. I got home too late last night to contact you. My timing was bad, I'm afraid. My apologies.'

He sounded as if he thought he was to blame and she hastened to reassure him. 'I should have telephoned first before calling at the castle, Mr Cullen. I'm sorry.'

He brushed her protestations aside. 'He sang your praises to the sky, did Harley. So . . . when can you start?'

'Oh,' she said in surprise. 'I thought you might want to interview me first.'

He gave a deep-throated laugh. 'I'll take Harley's word that you'll do, no question. I'm satisfied, if you are. Shall we say this morning at eleven sharp? Don't be late.'

And that was that. For a few moments after he rang off Shona gazed at her mobile in wonder and then glanced at the toby jug in his place on the passenger seat beside her, gazing impassively ahead. 'You don't care, do you?'

she said. 'You could at least show a bit of interest.'

She took another deep breath, marvelling at how quickly things changed. One minute she was thinking of the road ahead leading her into the unknown and now she knew exactly where she was going, back to Ferniehope Castle. There it seemed she would start her new life as personal assistant to Jack Cullen, owner of the conference centre.

Suddenly invigorated, she put the car into gear and started off again, hoping she was doing the right thing. Jack Cullen hadn't suggested coming for a trial period so they could both work out whether this was a good idea. He must trust Harley de Los implicitly. Suppose she didn't suit after all? Or didn't like the job? Well, she would soon discover that.

She drove straight there, bypassing Newton Stewart and reaching the main road before she knew it. Sunshine silvered the water of the estuary to her right and to her left the mountains were hazy against the pale sky. Nearly there . . . but, wait a minute, it was much too early. Keen she might be, but turning up an hour and-a-half before the appointed time wouldn't look at all good. Needy and pathetic, in fact. She imagined Jack Cullen's contempt and her own feeling of disadvantage.

She needed somewhere to spend the intervening time. Bessie's Kitchen, of course.

*   *   *

To her surprise a coach was parked in the yard at the side and a roar of laughter and chatter greeted her as she pushed open the door. A smiling Liz pouring coffee and cutting slices of carrot cake, waved to Shona. 'Be with you in a minute,' she mouthed.

Shona smiled as she seated herself at the table in the far corner. She had plenty of time to sit here watching all the people bustling about. Too much really. A stir of apprehension rippled through her because the time was getting nearer when she would meet the man she knew now was her future buss.

Gradually the noise subsided as everyone sat down and placed the remaining orders. Liz, looking a little harassed in spite of her outwardly calm manner, came to her. She was wearing blue today and her perfume was the same light fragrant one.

'I wasn't expecting an onslaught this early,' she said, smiling.

'Don't worry about me,' Shona said. 'You're busy and I don't need anything, just to kill a bit of time until I have to be at Ferniehope Castle. I've been offered the job there I told you about.'

'You have?' said Liz, looking surprised.

There it was again, Shona thought, that strange air of disquiet.

24

'Can I just sit here out of the way?'

'You're welcome, Shona. We'll talk some other time. Sorry it's so busy.'

'Good for business,' Shona murmured as Liz edged away. She had planned to ask her about Jack Cullen to find out what kind of a man he was apart from being good with a rake. He was obviously someone prepared to take a friend's recommendation on board and act on it quickly.

Running a conference centre held responsibilities so he must have a lot of experience gained over many years. She had already seen for herself that he was a confident man, completely sure of himself and his ability to cope with everything that such a position threw up.

She got up at last, checked she had her bag with her and then left. Liz, busy at the till, didn't see her go.

*   *   *

Turning into the drive to Ferniehope Castle today felt like coming home this time and that was a good sign surely? The sunny front of the building looked welcoming and she parked her car to one side and crunched across the gravel and up the short flight of stone steps.

Jack Cullen opened the door himself. She was expecting this but it was still a shock to see him dressed in a white shirt that looked as if it had been freshly ironed and his black brogues highly polished. He seemed older today, late thirties probably.

'Miss Renison, I do believe?' He took her hand in his and pressed it. 'Come in, come in. A good journey from whence you came this fine morning?'

Shona smiled. 'I enjoyed the drive.'

'That's good.'

He pressed a button on the desk in the large hall. 'Coffee for two, please, Ingrid, in the conservatory,' he ordered when a door at the far end opened.

Shona glanced about her, liking the comfortable feeling of dark furniture and velvet curtains. There was even an ample stone fireplace filled with fir cones with a tapestry screen to one side. The faint scent of roses lingered in the air. A new-scented furniture polish or had someone been spraying in here?

Jack Cullen turned to her. 'Shona . . . may I? And I'm Jack to everyone. Coffee first and then a guided tour. I'll fill you in on a few things while we drink it. OK with you?'

'Very much so,' she said.

He led the way to the conservatory that overlooked the sunny back lawn. Donald had done a good job with the mowing, she thought, but there was no sign of him today.

'Take a seat, Shona. Coffee won't be long.'

He waited until she seated herself in a creaking basket chair and then sat down opposite her. She glanced around her. The plants here in this shady conservatory looked well tended. She exclaimed in pleasure at the display of orchids on low tables out of the direct sunlight and at the white jasmine climbing against the glass walls. The sweet scent from it mingled with another richer one and was almost overpowering.

Jack looked at the orchids with pride. 'I've been collecting these for a while now,' he said. 'When I started out I didn't realise there were so many varieties.'

She smiled. 'I can see that someone loves them.'

'I've got some beauties like that Miltoniopsis over there, Red Knight.' His face shone with enthusiasm and for a moment she saw a softer side to him than the rather hard man who had first greeted her. He got up and smoothed the dark shiny leaves of the flamboyant orchid on the windowsill near her. 'This fellow likes a west facing position and what a scent he's got.'

'It's lovely,' said Shona.

'You like them too?' He leaned forward eagerly. 'I'm a bit of a fanatic on the quiet, but Ingrid keeps me in check.'

'Ingrid?'

'My secretary, Donald's daughter. Her mother, Mags, does the cooking and oversees the cleaning. They live in the cottage near the back gate. We employ other staff too as you'll see. But so far no one to act as hostess to the guests and that's why you're here.' He sounded as if he was pleased with himself for employing her. She hoped he wouldn't regret it.

There was a clatter of china and an exclamation of annoyance from the open doorway.

'Ah, here's Ingrid now.'

He took the laden tray from the sandy-haired girl who stood stolidly staring at them. 'Ingrid, this is Shona.'

Ingrid sniffed. 'Good morning,' she said in the same rasping tone as yesterday.

Jack placed the tray on one of the small bamboo tables and then sat down again. 'Thank you, Ingrid. That's great. You won't need to hang around much longer, but I'll need you to show Shona to her room before you head off.'

Ingrid threw Shona a look of dislike before she retreated.

'You'll welcome the conference delegates on arrival, Shona,' Jack said. 'See to their comfort in all matters and generally be at hand all the time they are here to deal with any problems that arise. How do you like your coffee?'

'White please, no sugar.'

She watched him pour and then took the mug from him, noticing the design of yellow orchids decorating it. As she put it down on the small bamboo table at her side she saw a

28

crack above the handle that he obviously hadn't noticed. His own, with a pink orchid appeared undamaged. Surely Ingrid hadn't made up her mind to dislike her before they had even met and was showing her in this small way that she was unwelcome here?

Jack proffered a plate of shortbread and then took one himself. He downed his coffee swiftly and she had the impression that her mini interview was over and that he had more important things on his mind now. Her mouth burning from the hot liquid, she drank as quickly as she could. He stood up as she replaced her empty mug on the tray.

*   *   *

Shona was expecting a small room to be allocated to her somewhere at the top of the building but the apartment Ingrid showed her on the first floor almost took her breath away.

'It's perfect,' she gasped, gazing in awe as Ingrid threw open the door to reveal a comfortably furnished sitting room in subtle shades of blue and green. Ingrid stumped across the pale green carpet to open the door into the bedroom.

Shona, following her, saw a patchwork quilt in various shades of pink edged with cream lace that matched the colour of the carpet. Deep rose velvet curtains framed the long window that, like the sitting room, looked out

29

over the front lawn.

'It'll do,' said Ingrid grudgingly.

Shona turned to her, smiling, but Ingrid's frosty expression didn't change. She edged towards the door. 'You'll need to find your own way down,' she said.

'No problem,' Shona said as Ingrid left her to explore the apartment on her own. She discovered pink towels in the ensuite and a selection of bath oil, shampoo and liquid soap on the glass shelf. Someone wanted her to feel welcome at Ferniehope Castle, but definitely not Ingrid.

'WHAT WILL HAPPEN TO HER?'

'Where are you now, Shona? Somewhere exotic . . . dining in style at Culzean Castle with Felix? Tell him from me to make the most of the present moment even though you've a lot of catching up to do.'

Shona laughed at her cousin's nonsense, glad that Jodie sounded happy and relaxed on the other end of the phone.

'I'm not too far from our old haunts,' she said, glancing out of the dining room window at the reddening sky behind the belt of trees to her right.

'So have you met Felix yet?'

'Of course not, Jodie. Be realistic.'

'You will, given time. I hope you're not thinking of moving on already?'

Shona smiled. 'No way. I'm enjoying myself too much.' And so she was, learning from Jack all that was expected of her. Not much today, of course, as the Roddon Rambling Club wasn't arriving until tomorrow and everything was in hand. It was just a question of familiarising herself with the layout of the castle and getting to know the rest of the staff. She had met Mags, Ingrid's mother, after lunch when she was investigating the rooms at the back of the house on the ground floor.

She had discovered her on her hands and knees wiping down the skirting board of the laundry room. Mags had struggled to her feet and held out her hand in welcome, a warm smile on her face. 'Pleased to meet you, lass. A fine place to work, Ferniehope Castle. Come and visit us in the cottage when you've settled in. We'd like that fine.'

No chilly reception here, Shona thought as she thanked her. But she would make quite sure that Ingrid was busy elsewhere before she took her up on her kind invitation.

'Are you still there?' said Jodie. 'Or just dreaming of your first meeting with you-know-who?'

Shona laughed and for the rest of the call concentrated on Jodie and her family. She was still smiling as she clicked off her mobile and slid it into the pocket of her long flowery skirt

31

she had changed into for her first evening meal at Ferniehope Castle.

Jack had told her that there were to be guests and she walked nimbly down the wide staircase in anticipation of a pleasant evening in their company. So far so good and tomorrow she might tell Jodie about this fabulous place and her job of personal assistant that she seemed to have found so easily.

*　　*　　*

'This is my personal assistant, Shona,' Jack said as he greeted his two elderly guests in the hall as she came down to join them.

He looked distinguished in his dinner jacket and she was glad she had put on her highest heels in honour of what she had been told was a special occasion.

But, oh horrors, in her haste she felt herself trip on the bottom step.

'Oh, my dear,' the tallest of the two elderly men had said in concern while the other rushed to support her, muttering soothing words.

For an embarrassed moment she leant against him, her face glowing. 'I'm sorry,' she gasped, regaining her balance. Glancing at Jack she saw him frown.

'My dear, are you all right?' her rescuer asked.

'Oh thank you, yes, of course,' she stuttered. What a bad first impression of someone who was here to represent Jack Cullen with the public as well as his personal friends, she thought. Elegant and poised she was not.

'Alfred Caruthers and his brother, James,' said Jack smoothly. 'Important people at Ferniehope, my mentors you might say. I couldn't have accomplished half of what I have here if it wasn't for the support of these two.'

He ushered them all into his private sitting room and offered drinks.

Shona accepted a glass of sherry and turned to James Caruthers who had taken the seat next to hers. The scent of roast lamb wafted in from the adjoining dining room and the old man sniffed in appreciation.

'Jack has the good sense to employ a first class cook,' he said. 'Just as he has when employing all his staff. A discerning chap is Jack. I'm glad to meet you, my dear.'

After the meal neither guest would hear of Shona retiring to give them some private time with their host.

'No, my dear young lady,' said Alfred Caruthers, his chair creaking as he settled himself comfortably. 'It's not often that two old codgers like us talk to a pretty young lady. Is that not right, James?'

'Indeed.'

Shona laughed, feeling herself blush. She gathered that they had known Jack a long time because they drifted off into reminiscences of when he had first discovered Ferniehope Castle. The place had been virtually a ruin then but Jack had seen the potential. Now, two years later, they were delighted with his achievements.

'Take no notice of the exaggerations of these two,' said Jack, smiling at her. 'Everyone has need of a fan club at some stage of their lives and that's what these two have been.'

James Caruthers shifted a little in his seat.

'The poor old lady who owned the place had let it go for years before she died,' he said. 'Her great nephew was difficult about the sale, I remember, and the legal side took a while to sort out. He accused Jack of all sort of perfidy. All nonsense, of course. The nephew's still bitter about it, I gather.'

Jack leaned back, looking supremely confident. 'I can deal with any bad feeling on his part,' he said.

'Don't be so sure of that, young man,' said Alfred. 'But we'll back you up if we need to.'

The evening passed pleasantly and Shona retired to her luxurious apartment feeling pleased with her first day.

*   *   *

'You'll find a print-out of the list of delegates on my desk,' said Jack, sticking his head round the breakfast room door as Shona was

34

finishing her meal next morning.

'Delegates?' she said.

'That's what we call all the guests who book in here for whatever reason,' he said. 'The members of the walking group in this case.'

'I see.'

'See to it, Shona, will you? I'll be away all day. Back at tea time.'

She scraped her chair back as she got up. 'Of course.'

He smiled. 'Your time is your own after that.'

He had gone by the time she thought to ask exactly what he meant her to do with the list. This morning he seemed distant and not a bit like the hospitable host of yesterday evening.

Ah well, she thought now, nothing for it but to find out for herself what she was supposed to do. Could this be some sort of initiative test? But no, she was certain that Jack Cullen wasn't the kind of person to set a trap like that. He was direct, straightforward. Blunt, even, sometimes. He had been kind, though, to his elderly friends, listening with patience to their rambling reminiscences.

She pushed open the office door and walked across to the desk in the window and found the list was where Jack had said it would be. She saw names down one side in a grid and across the top the names and numbers of rooms upstairs. Not too difficult to work out that her job was to match room numbers with

35

names.

She sat down in the swivel chair to study it, aware of the heady scent of grass cuttings floating in on the breeze from the open window. On the opposite wall was another window high up with a yellow orchid on the windowsill. Shona smiled to see it. Then she looked down at her notes again.

At last she looked up in frustration. Whoever thought these room names up must have been as crazy as she felt herself . . . *Shorter and Son, Pearly King, Pied Piper, Lord Mayor, Old King Cole, London Bobby, Big Ben, Mad Hatter* . . . all decidedly weird names for bedrooms.

She would have to go and investigate to check the ratio of single to double. They could all be single, of course, as this was a conference centre and not a luxury hotel, but she had better make sure.

On the first landing she tried the handle of the room labelled *Dombey and Son.* Locked of course, like the rooms on either side. She should have thought of that. Problems. Now what was she to do? No one was about downstairs. In fact the whole place had a feeling of emptiness about it.

She opened the front door and stood on the top step, considering. Not even the distant hum of a mowing machine filled the air, only some birdsong from the trees near the road. What would Jack expect her to do . . . just allocate the rooms willy-nilly? That could be fun but might have embarrassing consequences. A clue from the room names? Not really. *Pied Piper* could be a dormitory of bunk beds and *Jolly Jim* a room with an extra large mini bar. Or not.

She smiled, imagining the mistakes that could be made.

And how would she know if the men and women with the same surnames were even related to each other let alone married? There was the possibility here of messing things up big time. How Ingrid would love that!

She glanced once more at the trees at the bottom of the drive and saw the figure of a young girl flit furtively between them. Shona blinked and the girl was gone.

Returning to the office, she replaced the list on Jack's desk. Too bad it was Saturday and Ingrid wasn't at work. But her mother, Mags, would surely be in soon to see to lunch and could fill her in on what she wanted to know. Who better, really, to contact for help?

*   *   *

'A young girl?' said Mags, reaching into the cupboard for the scales and placing them with a thump on the large wooden table in the centre of the room. 'You saw her, you said?'

'I thought I did,' said Shona. 'A glimpse among the trees, that's all. I'll take a walk around when I've sorted the rooms unless you'd like some help here?'

'Not me,' said Mags comfortably. 'I'm getting some preparation done just now for the people coming in tomorrow.'

She looked as if she was set to enjoy herself for hours, her huge bulk clad in a long blue dress topped by a white apron. She seemed so much of part of the brightly cosy kitchen that Shona smiled.

'Lunch'll be at one today,' said Mags, pausing in what she was doing. 'So you've plenty of time to have a good look round at the rooms. Och, I'm surprised Ingrid hasn't allocated them all days ago. Jack will have expected her to have done it, I'm sure.'

Shona was surprised too, when she came to think of it. She took the master key to the rooms that Mags gave her and set off on a voyage of discovery. Mags had told her that although most of the rooms were single ones there was one double one on each floor.

'The married couples have those,' Mags had said. 'That'll be indicated on the booking forms.'

Which, of course, she hadn't got.

Checking the rooms took Shona longer than she had expected. Each one was decorated in different colours and she paused to admire the delicate water colour paintings that hung above each bed. The charming results of some of the painting courses, perhaps? Someone had taken a great deal of trouble with each room. Mags, probably. Lucky delegates staying in the place like this.

And of course she was lucky too.

Jack had told her to take a look around the area so when she had at last arranged the accommodation to the best of her ability, making a mental note to check that she had got it right about the double rooms, she went out into the fresh air of the morning determined to make the most of some free time. She hadn't seen the village of Ferniehope yet so that would be the first place to head for.

*   *   *

Shona saw her as soon as she reached the bottom of the drive. Startled, the girl leapt up from the bank that edged the road, letting fall a brown canvas bag with a heavy thud. Then, swaying for a second, she collapsed in a heap among last year's dead leaves the same colour as her tawny hair.

With a cry of alarm, Shona sprang to her. The girl stirred and sat up, rubbing her eyes.

'Are you OK?' Shona said. Stupid question. Of course she wasn't OK. 'Where have you come from? How long have you been here?'

'Don't fuss,' the girl mumbled as she staggered to her feet. Dressed in a short denim skirt and navy sweatshirt, she looked

39

dishevelled and had dark circles beneath her eyes.

'Fuss?' said Shona. 'Have some sense. You look terrible. What d'you expect me to do . . . walk straight past?'

The girl shrugged her thin shoulders.

'When did you last eat something?'

She seemed about sixteen, seventeen at the most, Shona thought. Too young anyway to be hanging round here looking as if she had spent all night out in the open.

'Come on, my place is near . . . the castle.'

'Oh no,' the girl murmured. 'Not there.' She looked haunted suddenly as if she was about to collapse again.

Shona looked up and down the road. No one was about, of course, when they were needed. 'No choice, I'm afraid,' she said firmly.

To her relief the girl picked up her bag and nodded.

*   *   *

In the kitchen Mags looked up from rolling out pastry. 'Back already? And I see we've got company. What are you doing here, Tamsin?'

'Mrs Mathieson,' said the girl.

'So you know each other,' said Shona pulling out a chair. 'Sit down,' she ordered.

'You know your dad's not here, Tamsin?' Mags said, continuing with her work.

40

'I do now.'

'She needs feeding,' said Shona, wondering at Mags' calm reception. 'Can I get her something?'

'All in good time,' said Mags. 'We'll phone that school of hers first and see if they'll take her back this time. The number's in the book by the phone on the dresser. What they're thinking of letting a fifteen-year-old girl wander off like this, I don't know.'

'Fifteen?' said Shona faintly. She looked at Tamsin closely. She could see now that the girl was younger than she had thought and her heart went out to her in her obvious unhappiness. 'You phone, Mags,' she said. 'While I find some bread and cheese for her. Is that OK?'

'Fine.'

'And I see the kettle's on the boil.'

Shona set about the preparations, glad of some immediate action. She could see that Mags was none too pleased to have Tamsin in her kitchen, but something had to be done.

She was longing to know where the girl had come from and what she was doing here.

Tamsin devoured the food Shona put in front of her and looked a lot better for it and for the mug of tea she was sipping at as Mags put down the receiver.

'That's that then,' she said in disapproval. 'I said someone would drive her back as soon as possible. I hope I did right. They'll get on to

41

that father of hers to say she's been found. They'll likely have notified the police.'

'Police,' said Tamsin so startled she upset some tea on the table. She banged the mug down, upsetting more.

Mags tut-tutted as she reached for a cloth. 'Questions need answering, lass. You'll not get off scot-free.'

Tamsin glared at her. 'I'll be dead.'

'I'll get my car keys,' said Shona. 'Come with me to my room first for a tidy up, Tamsin, and then I'll drive you back.'

Mags nodded. 'That'll be good.' She wrung her cloth out at the sink with her back to them, but Shona could see from the determined line of her shoulders that she was relieved to be shot of the responsibility.

Tamsin pushed her chair back and got to her feet. Her shoulders slumped as she followed Shona from the room.

*   *   *

Walking away and leaving Tamsin to the mercies of the dark-haired brittle-looking woman who was the head of the school where Tamsin had been a boarder for the past two years was incredibly difficult. What emotions seethed beneath the surface of that calm exterior? Fury, no doubt, and a real fear of the consequences for Benwood House if the press got hold of the story.

Miss Bowen greeted them kindly enough and at once rang the bell on her desk to summon the matron.

'We'll talk about this later, Tamsin,' she said as the girl was led away. Her tone of voice was pleasant but there seemed to be an undercurrent of something else that Shona found disturbing.

The headmistress turned to Shona as the door closed. 'And now I must thank you for returning Tamsin to us. You are a friend of the family?'

Shona hesitated. The direct gaze of the headmistress was daunting. 'I hope I will be one day,' she said. 'I'm a new employee at Ferniehope Castle, the conference centre run by Jack Cullen the owner. Apparently Tamsin arrived there last night expecting to find her father and then left when she found he wasn't there.

'I found her nearby this morning. That's all I can tell you, I'm afraid.'

Miss Bowen smiled, her plain face softening for a moment. 'This was kind of you, Miss Renison. I'm sure her father will be in touch in due course to thank you for caring for his daughter.'

'And the police?'

Miss Bowen's face seemed to freeze. 'The need to inform the police has now gone.'

'What will happen to her?'

'I'm afraid I can't say at the moment.'

And it was clear that Miss Bowen wasn't going to give anything away about her troublesome pupil, Shona thought, feeling snubbed.

'May I know your name and details?'

Shona gave them and then left, refusing refreshment. The sooner she was away from here the better. She could do nothing more for Tamsin now.

'YOU LOOK AS IF YOU'VE SEEN A GHOST'

Jack's car was parked in the yard at the back of the building when Shona got back to Ferniehope Castle. She glanced at her watch as she parked beside his vehicle. Four o'clock! She had phoned Mags as she was leaving Benwood House and then stopped for a coffee and a sandwich on the way back. Strangely, she had missed Tamsin's company.

To help make up for it she got Toby out of his hideaway in the glove compartment and put him back on the seat beside her. He was a silent passenger. Not much change there because Tamsin hadn't spoken much, only the odd bitter comment about people minding their own business and leaving her alone, which Shona had guessed referred more to Mags than herself.

44

'I don't tell her how to run her life,' Tamsin had muttered. 'And she wouldn't take any notice if I did. I'd make her get rid of those foul fridge magnets for a start.'

Smiling now at the memory Shona went into the hall and saw Jack standing by the telephone table with a book in his hand. 'Had a good day?' he asked.

Surprised at his critical tone she looked up at him. He had removed his jacket and tie but the expression on his face looked anything but relaxed. 'Well, yes . . .' she began.

'Your good deed for the day, I take it?'

'I'm sorry?'

'Mags put me in the picture. I don't approve of my employee chasing about the countryside on other people's business.'

'This was in my free time,' she reminded him.

'Even so. Interfering in what you must have known could be a police matter showed a severe lack of judgement on your part. I thought better of you than that, Shona. I expect total loyalty at all times from my staff.'

Shona was speechless. His attack was unfair and totally undeserved. What had she done other than show some common humanity?

His direct gaze was daunting. 'I need your promise that it won't happen again.'

'I hope it won't,' said Shona, finding her voice at last. 'But I can't give that promise.'

'That's not good enough.'

45

Shona stared back at him. 'I did what I thought was right at the time. I still do.'

'That's a matter of opinion.'

'My opinion,' said Shona firmly.

Jack shut the book and put it down on the table. 'Dinner's at seven,' he said. 'Don't be late.'

Shona nodded. She had felt hungry a moment ago but not now.

'And before I forget. Felix Langholme? He's flying home tonight. Don't look like that, Shona. He's not blaming you. Why should he? Shona, are you all right?' His voice softened. 'You look as if you've seen a ghost.'

She felt as if she had. 'Are you sure?'

'For goodness sake, girl. What's got into you?'

She put out a hand to steady herself against the hall table. 'The name . . . I knew someone once with that name. He lived near here.'

'Then you'll know that he's totally unreliable, swanning off abroad when he feels like it and letting someone else take care of his responsibilities.'

'I knew him when we were children.'

'I don't suppose he'll have changed much since then,' said Jack in a tone of dismissal.

*   *   *

Too impatient to wait for the tide to go out, she waded through water as thick as honey to reach the island. Strangely, she arrived on the shore on the other side bone-dry.

Waking suddenly from her dream, Shona didn't know at first where she was and still felt the warm sand beneath her body instead of the soft mattress of her bed at Ferniehope Castle.

Outside it was light and she could hear birdsong. Vestiges of sheer happiness lingered and she felt as she had all those years ago at the thought of spending another day in Felix's company.

Now she took a deep breath and let it out slowly to acclimatise herself to being safe in her bedroom instead of having spent the night in the open air as poor Tamsin had done the night before.

When Jack had told her that Felix Langholme was on his way home from somewhere far away, Shona had been too surprised to question why he had told her this. It was only as she was getting ready for bed hours later that she realised that the two events were connected. Too late then to ask Jack to fill in the details. In his mood of last evening she wasn't sure that it would have been a good idea anyway.

Tamsin's absent father was Felix Langholme, whom she had known as a boy long ago.

Now, early as it was, Shona sat up. She needed to be up and dressed and ready to face whatever today had in store.

47

*   *   *

The first members of Ruddon Ramblers arrived early but Shona was ready for them, clipboard in hand.

A moment later the bell rang with a determined sound that echoed round the hall.

Shona opened the door, smiling. On the doorstep were three men and a woman, clad in shorts and bulky jackets. No one could mistake them for being other than an enthusiastic walking group eager to start out on their first trek and prepared to be pleased with everything.

'Coffee will be served in the dining room,' she said when the introductions were made and she located their names on the list she was holding.

Involved as she was with making sure everyone knew which rooms they were allotted, Shona wasn't aware that there was a stranger among them until someone asked why the bedrooms had such strange names.

'I can answer that,' said someone behind her.

She swung round.

His eyes twinkled at her. 'Felix Langholme.'

'Tamsin's father,' she said faintly. He was wearing jeans and a navy crew-necked sweater beneath a denim jacket. He hadn't recognised her. Even though she knew it was unlikely

48

after all these years she felt a stirring of disappointment.

'I'd like to be of help if you'll allow me.'

'Of course.'

'Good morning all,' he said with a flourish.

Smiling greetings were returned and Shona could see the effect of his charm. He had an easy confidence that had been lacking in the rather diffident young lad she had come to know so well long ago. She wondered where Tamsin's mother was and where Felix lived now.

'So you are able to tell us?' said the man who had asked the question. 'The room names sound decidedly odd to me.'

'You've heard of character jugs?'

'Toby jugs?'

'This place used to be full of them. The owner was a collector.'

'So they called the rooms after the jugs?' said the man, light dawning.

'So where are they all now?' a young woman in a frilly dress and hiking boots demanded, looking around as if she expected a gang of toby jugs to materialise on tables and chairs.

'You tell me.'

There were further questions and in the flurry of more arrivals Shona was kept busy. Her concentration on remembering everything that Jack expected of her was exhausting. Where was he, anyway?

When at last she was free she came

downstairs again with an apology on her lips for leaving Felix to his own devices. She found him in the conservatory looking critically at one of Jack's pale lemon orchids.

'This needs attention,' he said sternly as if its drooping appearance was her fault.

'May I offer you some coffee?' she said.

'Look at this wretched thing.'

'I'd rather not. I'm sure Jack's got its welfare in hand.'

He turned, smiling, towards her. 'Miss Renison?'

She could see he still didn't remember her. Twenty years was a long time after all and his mind would be focussed on the present situation.

'It seems I have you to thank for restoring my daughter to her rightful place,' he said.

'Rightful?' Shona couldn't keep the doubt out of her voice.

'You question that?'

'It's none of my business, but . . .'

'Too right,' said Jack Cullen from behind her. 'I'm not sure I like my employee mixed up in all this, Felix. You must sort out your own problems. Shona's here to work for me.'

Felix looked at Jack steadily, his right hand clenched. 'I came merely to thank her for showing compassion and kindness to Tamsin when she needed it. Is that such a bad thing?'

Jack made no answer but with an exclamation of dismay, moved across to the windowsill and bent to examine the wilting orchid. He straightened. 'Who did this?'

'Are you accusing me?' Felix's voice was rough and Shona couldn't blame him. 'Not guilty, I'm afraid. Try Shona! Or Ingrid!' His face brightened. 'Is Ingrid anywhere around?'

Ignoring his question, Jack glanced at his watch. 'I think you should leave. I need to do some first aid here. Shona, carry on with the arrangements, will you. I'll see everyone later.'

'Yes, of course.' She tried to sound confident.

Felix turned to her, his voice softening. 'I think I must leave my thanks until another time.'

'You do that,' said Jack as he turned to go. 'Shona has work to do.'

'I'll be in touch, Shona, when things have quietened down,' said Felix. 'A meal away from here perhaps?'

'That would be good,' she said, pleased.

*   *   *

The leader of Ruddon Ramblers, a short stocky man with receding hair, had the programme for the week in his hand when he came to find Shona in the office after lunch.

'We're more or less settled in now Jeannie's room had been changed,' he told her, shuddering. *'Henry the Eighth* . . . I don't think so. Nor for Jeannie. *Anne Hathaway* is much

51

better and she's pleased you could sort it out.'

'That's good,' said Shona, smothering a laugh. Luckily there was a spare room available of exactly the same proportions as the disliked one. It would really have been easier to have changed the name plates had that been possible.

'I see afternoon tea is scheduled for four o'clock today. I'd like to organise a walk round the grounds now. Could you put tea back for an hour?'

'No problem at all, Mr Luttrell. I'll see to it at once.'

His small eyes gleamed at her. 'Rex,' he said. 'Call me Rex.'

'Fine, Rex,' Shona said, hoping Mags wouldn't be put out by the new arrangement.

Ingrid was in the kitchen with her mother when Shona went to find out.

'It's too bad of you to change the programme,' Ingrid burst out. 'We can't have this sort of thing I hope you told him so.'

'It seemed a reasonable request,' said Shona.

'And so it is,' said Mags, her cheerful face a contrast to her daughter's grimmer one. 'Be off with you, Ingrid, and leave us to get things sorted here.'

Ingrid's mouth was a thin line and the look she threw Shona was venomous. 'I'll go then. I can see when I'm not wanted.'

'Take no notice of her,' said Mags when she

52

had gone. 'She gets in a strop when she can't get her own way, right enough. It'll blow over. We've time for a cup ourselves now that their tea is put back. Sit down, lassie, and take the weight off your legs. Not that you've got any spare weight of course, not like me.'

She sounded so complacent that Shona laughed. The atmosphere had lightened because of Mags and the kitchen felt a friendly place. There was still the evening's programme to feel apprehensive about, though, but for the moment she could relax.

*   *   *

Jack gave a welcome speech when the group gathered with their coffee in the lounge after dinner. He spoke movingly about the attractions for walkers in the surrounding area and promised an interesting week at Ferniehope Castle.

'You did well earlier,' he said to Shona when he had finished. 'Everything seems on course for the programme tomorrow. Donald will bring the minibus to the front door at ten. Whitborn Abbey and the Machars, a shortish walk. The forecast is OK with sunny periods. Mags knows about the packed lunches?'

Shona nodded. 'It's all in hand. They know where to leave their boots and outdoor clothing when they get back. Rex, Mr Luttrell, was please to find there's a drying room next door.'

'It's stated clearly—the specifications.' Jack raised an eyebrow and his lips twitched. 'Perhaps he can't read?'

She smiled. 'He was able to read the name plates on the bedroom doors.'

'Just as well or the written sheets for the quiz this evening would be lost on him. We'll both be on duty as it's their first night but then we'll take it in turns to be here, starting with you tomorrow. Is that all right?'

'Of course.'

'Good girl. It's good to have you here.'

She glowed at his praise.

He looked at her closely. 'A word of warning, Shona. I don't want to see you hurt. You've done enough for that man. Don't be fooled by his so-called charm.'

No need to ask which man he had in mind. 'I won't,' she promised.

'I know him of old. Please be sensible and have nothing more to do with him.'

She smiled but didn't answer.

INGRID SHOWS HER TRUE COLOURS

Ferniehope Castle was very quiet after the group's noisy departure next morning with much laughter and banging of doors. Shona wandered from room to room checking that no one had left anything lying around they might not be able to find later. She gave Jack's office a wide berth because she knew Ingrid was working in there, finalising next week's programme for the group of wildlife enthusiasts.

In the guests' lounge she found the pile of completed quiz sheets laced neatly on the piano lid. On the top was the one marked with Jeannie's name in a flowery scrawl. She had got top marks. Rex's effort was at the bottom. Smiling, Shona left them where they were.

She heard the telephone's ring from the hall and paused as Ingrid stuck her head round the office door.

'It's for you,' she said abruptly.

'I'll take it in the dining room,' said Shona.

She was glad she had because the voice on the end was Felix's.

'This evening?' he said. 'Any good? Bessie's Kitchen is doing a curry night. D'you like curry?'

'I'm sorry, Felix,' she said, a catch of disappointment in her voice. 'I'm on duty here.'

'That's too bad. Can't you just slip out without anyone noticing?'

'You know I can't. It's more than my job's worth.'

'Then get another.'

'As easily as that? I don't think so.'

'OK, then, how about if I get Bessie to put

on a special curry when you and I can actually get there?'

'Liz,' she said.

'Yes, Liz, of course. You know her?'

'A little. I'd love that, Felix. I'm so sorry about tonight.'

'Got paper and pen handy? I'll give you my number.'

'I'll remember it,' she said with confidence. If she didn't Jodie would be at her throat. 'But I'll write it down just in case. And thanks.'

She replaced the receiver, and before she forgot put the number he had given her on to her mobile.

The phone rang again, but this time Ingrid dealt with it in the office.

Later, when Shona came in from the garden with a bunch of daffodils to arrange in the empty lounge fireplace she was surprised to find Ingrid waiting for her.

'Oh hello,' she said. 'Did you want me?'

Ingrid looked at her quickly and then away again. 'About tonight. You're free if you want. Jack just phoned. He'll be here himself after all. No need for both of you to be.'

'Great. Thanks, Ingrid.' Shona felt light-hearted as she put the flowers in position and pulled out her mobile to phone Felix. Already her mind was on what to wear if his invitation was still on. Her new skirt and the cream and burgundy top. Medium heels would be best and her new drop earrings.

She changed her mind only once and that was to substitute the skirt for a pair of jeans. When she was at last ready she picked up her bag, slipped her mobile into it and took one last look in the mirror to check her hair.

*   *   *

Felix was waiting for her in the car park and together they went into the warm and lively atmosphere of Bessie's Kitchen. Liz's curry night was obviously popular and there was just one vacant table.

'Lucky us,' said Felix as he pulled out Shona's chair for her. They both selected vegetable biryani, a speciality of the house.

'Liz seems to be in her element,' Shona said, waving to her across the room.

'She's done wonders with this place,' said Felix.

'D'you often eat here?'

'Now and again. It's Tamsin's favourite.'

'Have you heard from her? How is she?'

He looked troubled. 'She's unhappy, I know that. I don't know what to do as I'm away so much. I really am grateful to you for looking after her, you know. I wish I could do something for you to show my appreciation.'

'There's no need,' she said quickly.

Their food arrived and Felix picked up his fork. Before Shona could do the same her mobile rang. 'Please excuse me, Felix,' she said. 'I meant to turn it off.'

'Don't mind me.'

Hastily she scrabbled in her bag and saw that the caller was Jodie. Smiling, she held the phone to her ear.

'Oh Shona, it's me,' said Jodie, her voice shaking.

Shona felt an icy chill though the room was warm. 'Jodie, what's wrong? What's happened?'

'It's Duncan. He had an accident. He . . . he's broken his ankle.'

'Broken his ankle? Where are you?'

'At the hospital.'

'Which hospital? Is he all right?'

'They've operated on him and his leg's in thick plaster all the way up. They're keeping him in tonight.'

'D'you want me to come back? I can be there in . . . '

'No, oh no. You can't do anything here, Shona. No one can. I just thought you ought to know, that's all. He'll be out of action for weeks. I don't know what we're going to do.'

'You'll stay living exactly where you are, Jodie, until it suits you to move into a place of your own.'

'But you'll have to come back after your holiday and get another job and you'll need us out of your apartment.'

'Listen, Jodie.' Speaking earnestly, Shona leaned forward as if Jodie was sitting across the table instead of Felix poised with his fork halfway to his mouth. 'I've got myself a job here. It's live-in, so your accommodation's not an issue. I'll fill you in on the details tomorrow. Promise.'

'So we really don't need to worry about the apartment?' The surprise and relief in her cousin's voice made Shona smile.

'A crisis?' said Felix as she clicked off her phone.

'That was my cousin, Jodie,' she said. 'You probably remember her.'

He raised his eyebrows. 'Should I?'

Shona picked up her fork. 'She was the little girl who liked to follow us about.'

'Sorry, you've lost me.'

For a confused moment she wondered if he was the same Felix Langholme that she had known years before. Laying down her fork, she stared at him.

'Would you like us to leave?' he said. 'You're obviously in shock, Shona.'

'No, it's not that. You don't remember me so of course nothing makes sense. Those holidays twenty years ago . . . I was the bigger girl, Shona Renison.'

'Shona Renison by all that's wonderful.'

She laughed shakily. 'You remember now?'

'I should think I do.' He leaned forward eagerly. 'I can hardly believe it. Dare I say you've grown into a beautiful woman? I never thought we'd meet again and now here you are. But something bad's happened?'

'Jodie's husband's broken his ankle,' she said.

'And they're keeping him in hospital overnight? I heard that much, Shona. But that's a good thing. Lets him rest where they can keep an eye on him.'

Felix's voice was so sympathetic that Shona felt ashamed of her initial panic. She began to eat again, scooping up mouth-watering morsels of aubergine steeped in rich sauce. 'This is one of the best biryanis I've ever eaten,' she said.

Felix looked pleased. 'That's the spirit. So, tell me about this Jodie I'm supposed to remember.'

Shona smiled. 'It feels like a fairy tale. I can see you're the same Felix as you were then. D'you remember joining in our games over on the island? We had some fine times and you were part of them.'

'Leckie Shore,' he said, the light of memory shining in his eyes.

She smiled. 'I'm glad to be back.'

'So Jodie was that little girl and you were . . . Shona. Yes, yes, yes!' He laughed with pleasure.

She felt her cheeks glow as they talked about those far-off days, finding so much to reminisce about that time stood still.

'We're practically related,' he said when Liz had removed their empty plates and produced the dessert menu.

He looked pleased about that but she wasn't so sure. He had been something more, something special. But that was then. She was here with him now enjoying this meal because he wished to show his gratitude to her for taking his daughter back to school. Nothing more.

As they ate their lemon cheesecake he filled her in with a few details of his own life, his studies at Falmouth Art College where he specialised in ceramics, the chance he had after he left to work with a firm in Cornwall where he met his future wife. And the agony of losing her in childbirth and his decision to move back north where he had family connections to help him bring up his young daughter until she was old enough to board at a suitable school.

Shona wanted to ask more about Tamsin, why she had run away and what the school was going to do about it, but felt it was too personal. He would tell her if he wanted her to know. 'And the work you do now?' she asked instead.

He smiled. 'I must show you my workshop one day. I'm a one-man band working at my designs and ceramics all hours with clients abroad I need to see periodically. That's why I have to be away from home so much. It's a living. How about you? Have you always done similar work as you're doing now?'

She told him of her work as a researcher and of how Jodie had been so supportive through the years of looking after her father.

'That's why I feel I must be there for her now,' she said, suddenly downcast.

'You're a good and generous girl,' said Felix warmly. Shona felt herself flush at his praise.

They ordered coffee and Liz came to join them bringing an extra cup with her. The other diners had gone now.

'No rush,' said Liz, pouring for them all. 'It's good to see you both.'

Shona leaned back in her chair. Jodie's news didn't seem quite so terrible now. She would phone tomorrow and find out all the details. And Jodie would want to hear about the new life she was forging for herself here and how the meeting with Felix had come about.

Shona smiled at him as he teased Liz about drinking away her profits, glad that she had found two such good friends. And she was thankful, too, that she had slotted into a job at Ferniehope Castle with accommodation provided so that Jodie and family had one less worry at this difficult time.

Dusk was beginning to fall by the time they left Bessie's Kitchen and their cars were the only ones in the car park.

Felix took a deep breath. 'I can smell salt and reeds and mud and all things wonderful,' he said, his head thrown back.

Shona laughed at him. 'What an imagination!'

'Superb, don't you think?'

'If you say so.'

They reached her car.

'I see you have company.'

Startled, she looked inside. 'Oh, you mean Toby.'

'He's got a name?'

She clicked on her key tab and opened the passenger door. 'He keeps me company.'

'Mind if I have a look?'

'Feel free' She reached inside and handed Toby to him. He turned the jug over in his hand and was silent for so long she felt alarmed. 'Is anything wrong?'

'Where did you get this?'

'Why do you ask?'

'He's the twin of one my aunt had.'

'She had one just the same? I discovered this among my father's possessions. I'm not sure I like thinking Toby's got a brother. I thought he was all mine.'

Felix laughed suddenly. 'He might be an only child now. My aunt's collection was split up when she died and a lot sold. He could be anywhere . . . broken, dead and buried in the mud down there at Leckie Shore.'

She laughed too. 'So you're not going to kidnap my Toby?'

'I wish I could.' He sounded serious but his eyes were dancing as he handed him back

63

to her.

*   *   *

Instead of leaving Toby in the car Shona carried him carefully into the house. Because of Felix's interest he had taken on a value for her he hadn't possessed before. He needed looking after even though the expression on his ugly face seemed smugger now than it had before.

'You'd better watch it,' she warned him. 'One false move from you and you are out there in the glove compartment in solitary confinement.'

Smiling, she shut the front door behind her and then hesitated, surprised to see Ingrid hovering in the hall dressed in a long black skirt and skimpy top. Surely not waiting for her? She glanced up at the clock on the wall above the desk. Twenty minutes to midnight.

Shona felt a shimmer of alarm. 'Something's wrong?'

'Why should there be?'

As Shona began to head towards the staircase Ingrid moved to block her way. 'I thought I'd check you were back before I left,' she said in a voice that sounded more rasping than usual.

Shona stifled a yawn. Ingrid was playing games but she wasn't going to join in. 'It's getting late,' she said.

64

Ingrid made no move to let her pass. 'Jack came back.'

'And?'

'You weren't here.'

'Did he want me then? You had my mobile number.'

Ingrid rubbed her hands up and down her bare arms as if she was suddenly cold. 'I suppose.'

'He can't have expected to see me, Ingrid, can he?'

'Maybe. Maybe not.'

Shona stared at her, suspicion stirring. 'Are you telling me you made it up about Jack giving me his last-minute permission to leave the place for the evening?'

'What if I did?' A smile hovered on Ingrid's lips and there was no doubting the pleasure she was taking in this exchange.

Shona took a painful breath. 'Ingrid, tell me, did you tell Jack where I was?'

'I don't give my friends away.'

'What sort of an answer's that?'

'Good enough for the time being.'

Shona clenched her hands until they hurt. Ingrid's words sounded like a threat. 'I can't believe you did that,' she said. 'I've never done you any harm.'

'No?' For a moment Ingrid stood motionless staring bleakly at Shona. Then she turned and left, fading away like a bad spirit intent on harm.

Shona went up to her rooms, regretting her stupidity in taking Ingrid's word for something she could have checked for herself. Jack wasn't the kind of person to change his mind when he had decided on a course of action.

With a heavy heart she got ready for bed. When at last she was beneath the duvet she curled into a ball for comfort and tried not to dwell on what might be ahead of her in the morning.

'DON'T GET INVOLVED, SHONA.'

Jack greeted Shona with a smile as she went into the office after breakfast. He looked so relaxed in his open-necked shirt, leaning back in his swivel chair, that it seemed that her fears were unfounded and Ingrid hadn't yet told him that she was absent last evening. But she would, oh yes she would. The question was . . . when?

'You're bright and early this fine morning,' he said indicating the nearest chair.

Shona sat down, smoothing the soft material of her skirt over her knees. 'Eager to start work, you see,' she said, smiling.

She saw that he had left off his gold watch today. The white skin on his wrist seemed to glimmer in the sunshine that filtered in through the broad open windows. A soft breeze stirred the curtains. She seemed to smell the sea on it, salt with a hint of mud. Ridiculous, of course, but there it was.

'Ingrid's been telling me . . .'

'What?' Her voice was sharper than she had intended and she swallowed hard in confusion.

He looked at her in concern. 'Are you all right, Shona?'

She struggled to take a hold on herself. 'Sorry,' she said faintly. 'I didn't sleep too well, that's all.'

'Any particular reason?'

'I'll get an early night tonight.'

He seemed satisfied. 'Taking on a new job can be tiring, I know.'

Shona smiled and agreed. What made it extra tiring, of course, was worrying that you might lose your job because someone else had set you up.

'It seems that the Ruddon Ramblers need some input from us,' Jack said. He picked up a pen, clicked it open and then put it down again. 'As you know they booked in for accommodation and meals to include packed lunches. And for transport to and from locations each day in the minibus. I understood that they had planned their routes in advance. Maybe they want to change and need advice.'

'You'd like me to deal with it?'

'D'you know much about planning suitable walking routes?'

'Well no,' she admitted.

He laughed. 'Nor me. A fine pair, aren't we? The trick is to appear confident as if you have all the knowledge they require at your pretty fingertips. I know I can rely on you, Shona.'

If only, she thought.

'Make sure you don't send them down dangerous precipices or up impossible heights and you'll be all right. How are your map reading skills?'

'Adequate, I think,' she said.

'Good girl.' He leaned forward and picked up a list. 'I'd like you to look at this. I've jotted down some figures here about arrivals the week after next. See to the arrangements, will you, Shona?'

She took the list he handed to her.

'Ingrid will have the list of food allergies and requirements,' he added. 'For a group of open air addicts they seem singularly unhealthy.'

Shona smiled. This morning Jack seemed a different person from the man who had greeted her on her arrival last Saturday. He had been friendly, but she had the feeling that she was being weighed in the balance. Hopefully his relaxed manner now meant he had accepted her. She determined to do all she could to make herself indispensable.

'I'll see you at lunchtime then, Shona.'

'I'll look forward to it,' she said. After

68

Ingrid's fun and games she would be on tenterhooks not knowing when the blow would strike. She was well aware that when it did she would have to explain to Jack exactly what had occurred even though Ingrid would lie through her teeth. Her word against Ingrid's. No prizes for guessing the outcome.

In the hall Shona paused for a moment to appreciate the delicate scent of invisible roses. Even after so short a time she felt completely at home here in Ferniehope Castle as if she had lived in a place like this all her life. Having to leave Jack's employ now would be shattering not only because Jodie would no longer have peace of mind but also on her own account.

*   *   *

Rex, flushed with importance, knelt down and spread his Ordnance Survey map of the area out on the dining room floor.

'I thought we'd explore the Galloway Forest Park today,' he said.

Shona smiled. 'Not all of it surely? D'you have a particular place in mind?'

'I thought you would tell me that,' he said simply. 'Isn't that what you're here for?'

'I'll do my best,' she said, squatting down close enough to examine the map. What luck that she had taken the trouble to read as much about the area as she could and knew a little

69

about the various Visitor Centres and where they were situated in the area of nearly three hundred square miles of forest, mountain and loch.

'I've put some leaflets on the table in the sitting room for you,' she said. 'How far do you want to walk today?'

Rex sat back on his heels and scratched his head. 'I'm not too sure about that.'

She looked at him in exasperation. 'I can get more information from the internet for you,' she said. 'But it'll take time and Donald has been told to have the minibus ready for you at ten o'clock, I believe. He can't be any later than that because he's due in Newton Stewart this morning.'

Rex folded the map and struggled to his feet. 'You'll be coming with us of course?'

She hid her surprise. 'Well no. I have work to do here today, Rex. I can't leave it.'

'Tomorrow then?'

'I think Jack will have to decide that. It's not down to me. Why don't you take your group off to somewhere like Culzean Castle today and do some walking in the country park there?'

'I suppose.'

She pointed to Glen Trool Visitor Centre on the map. 'That would be a good place to head for tomorrow. Plenty of marked trails and lots of other things too. I'll get all the information I can while you're away and print

70

it out for you. You'll have time this evening to plan some good routes and discuss them with the others. It's wonderful walking country.'

For a moment he looked undecided but then his face cleared. 'That sounds good,' he said. 'Thank you, my dear. You've been most helpful.'

*   *   *

At lunchtime Shona explained to Jack about Rex's planning problems as they ate their quiche and salad at a table Mags had laid for them in the conservatory. At this time of day the sunshine slanted in through the beech trees at the side of the house and reflected on the copper pots on the shelves at one end.

'You did well,' Jack said. 'He's a bit of an awkward customer, is Rex.'

'He expected me to go with them today.'

'He did? Would you have liked that?'

She shook her head. 'I got the feeling I'd be in charge and expected to lead.'

He laughed. 'Outside the call of duty, I think.'

'I'll get more pleasure researching the Forest Park on the website for him and doing some print-outs so he can plan his own itinerary.'

'Much the best way,' Jack agreed, helping himself to more salad. 'Better yet, how about doing it in person? I'd like a drive out to Glen

71

Trool myself. Shall we do that this afternoon?'

He looked at her keenly, the salad servers poised over the bowl. 'What do you say? What could be better on a glorious day like this?'

She smiled and agreed and for the rest of the meal they discussed the kind of information most useful to Rex. Shona leaned back in her chair, aware of the pleasantness of her surroundings among Jack's lovely orchids. The scented one wasn't so obvious today. In fact she couldn't see it in its place on the shady windowsill. She looked up higher.

'What's wrong?' said Jack, leaning back too so he could follow her gaze. 'Oh, you've seen the toby jugs.'

Startled, she looked again and saw several small jugs the same size as Toby tucked well back on their high shelf as if hiding from public gaze.

'I didn't notice them the other day,' she said. 'So my Toby has some friends here.'

'You like toby jugs?'

'I didn't know I did until I found him in my late father's china cabinet. I brought him with me for company, as a sort of mascot. I've grown fond of him.'

He gave her a quizzical look. 'We'll have to introduce them one of these days.'

'He'd like that,' she said with equal seriousness.

'These are just a small remnant of the collection that was here when I bought the place. I had some idea of having one in each bedroom, but it was pointed out to me that they might not be in residence for long.'

'You mean they'd get pinched?'

He smiled. 'It happens.'

'So you named the bedrooms after each toby jug instead?'

'Bright girl.'

'I can't imagine anyone with Rex's figure swarming up a ladder to reach one of those,' she said.

He laughed as he pushed his chair back and got up. 'All set then? Let's go.'

*   *   *

Shona couldn't remember when she had enjoyed an afternoon so much. Jack was a good driver and as they sped towards the hills she felt her worries lifting. She wished they could drive on forever towards the distant mountains outlined against the cerulean sky.

Even when Jack turned off and they were among the shadow of trees she was still aware of the hint of higher ground lurking further off. She could see that there was plenty of scope here for a variety of outdoor activities as well as the walking that Rex and his group wished to do.

'Excellent bird watching country,' said Jack. 'Most of Britain's raptors can be seen here.'

She murmured her surprise, not liking to

profess her ignorance. She'd get herself into the book room when they got back and consult a handy dictionary.

He glanced at her sideways, a smile on his lips. 'Know what they are?'

She felt herself flush. 'Birds?'

'Not bad. You need to be more specific though. Birds of prey. Buzzards are fairly common and if you're very lucky you might spot a golden eagle.'

The car park was half empty and Jack parked his vehicle in the shade. They got out and walked to the Information Centre.

'You'll have seen we have a group of birdwatchers booked in at Ferniehope in a few weeks' time,' Jack said. 'They come every year. This year they'll be concentrating on the Galloway Kite Trail.'

'Kites?' she said in surprise.

'You know that those superbly graceful birds were saved from extinction by one of the world's longest running protection programmes?'

'I don't know anything about them at all,' she admitted.

'They've been successfully re-introduced to Scotland and England now,' he said with satisfaction.

'That's great,' she said. She felt like asking why they had become extinct in the first place but she had come to the best place to find out if the number of information leaflets on the subject was anything to go by.

'Now that's a group you might like to join on your day off,' he said. 'They'd be glad to have you, I know. Ingrid's well in with them. Have a word with her.'

'I'll do that,' she said.

Away from Ferniehope Castle the mention of Ingrid's name cast no shadow on her enjoyment and when Jack suggested they move on to Clatteringshaws Visitor Centre for Shona to see for herself what it had to offer she agreed at once. Laden down with information about the various forest trails in the area as well as the many other activities they returned to the car, well pleased with the afternoon so far.

*　　　*　　　*

'That's that then,' Jack said as they turned into the drive of Ferniehope Castle. 'Enjoy yourself?'

'I had no idea that lovely area was so vast,' Shona said. 'Or so beautiful.'

'It's a very special place,' said Jack. 'We must do it again sometime.'

They reached the yard at the rear to park in Jack's usual place. As he got out of the vehicle the lines deepened on his forehead. 'Ingrid's car's not here,' he said. 'I hope there's some explanation.' He sounded worried.

Shona, following him inside the building,

was reminded instantly of how it could be if he discovered that she was absent from her post yesterday evening. But surely Ingrid had no need to worry? She was a long-established employee and daughter of his trusted retainers living with them in a cottage in the grounds. He couldn't run the place without a secretary.

Jack opened the office door and then closed it again, still frowning. 'I'll check with Mags,' he said.

Shona hesitated. 'Is there anything I can do?'

He shrugged. 'Not really. You'll have enough to do sorting through that lot. I'll see you at dinner time.'

She slipped away, clutching her pile of leaflets and brochures, and ran lightly up to her apartment, wanting to retain the euphoria of a wonderful afternoon for a while longer.

*   *   *

Her mobile rang.

'Shona.' Jack's voice was terse.

'Is something wrong?'

'I've just been on to Ingrid. D'you know Bessie's Kitchen?'

'Bessie's Kitchen? Well yes. But . . .'

'The girl's there, Felix Langholme's daughter. D'you know anything about this?' He sounded accusing.

'But why didn't Liz phone Tamsin's father?'

76

'I'm not getting involved in any of this, Shona. All I know is that her father has gone off somewhere, but no one knows where.'

'But I was with him yesterday evening and . . .' She paused, horrified, wishing she could have bitten her tongue off before she came out with something so stupid. Now what had she done?

'You shouldn't be mixed up in this, Shona. It's not your problem. Just leave well alone.'

'I'll telephone Liz and find out the details.'

'Do that if you must,' Jack said. 'And join me in the office when you've done it.'

She did nothing for a moment but stared down at her mobile, her thoughts whirling. She had condemned herself out of her own mouth. Jack would be waiting to hear exactly why she had deserted her post when he had left her in charge and she must face the consequences. But first there was Tamsin to consider.

She dialled the number Felix had given her. He answered at once. 'Felix Langholme.'

At the sound of his deep reassuring voice tears sprang to her eyes. 'It's Shona. Felix, where are you? There's a problem.'

'There is? Wait a minute, I'll turn off the TV.'

She had a moment to think of what to say so she didn't sound accusing. 'Have you heard from Liz at Bessie's Kitchen? It seems that Tamsin has shown up there and you couldn't be contacted.'

He gave an easy laugh. 'So that's where she is? I was supposed to meet her at the station but she wanted to be independent and get herself home to Crag Cottage on her own.'

'You were expecting her?'

'Measles at the school. They've been sent home. I'll go and collect her now. And thanks.'

He clicked off his phone.

Shona went downstairs where Jack met her in the doorway of the office.

'Everything sorted?' he said. 'So what happened?'

'Nothing happened,' she said. 'Her father was expecting Tamsin. He's gone to pick her up now. He was at home.'

'A false alarm then?'

'So it seems.'

He smiled. 'As I said, don't get involved, Shona. Obviously there was a mix-up somewhere along the line.'

She said nothing. Mix-up hardly described a deliberate ploy on Ingrid's part to stir up trouble. It was incredible that Jack hadn't worked out something of the sort himself.

Incredible, too, that he hadn't picked up on her admission that she had been with Felix when she should have been here at Ferniehope Castle.

JACK COMES TO RELY ON SHONA

'Here you are, lass,' said Liz, placing a glass of her favourite Coke and lemonade on the blue and white-checked tablecloth in front of Tamsin. 'He won't be long.'

Tamsin leaned forward to pick up her glass, her loose hair falling over her face. 'Thanks, Liz.'

The older woman relaxed a little. 'It really is true that there's this epidemic at your school, Tamsin. It's not just one of your tall stories?'

'Lies you mean?'

'No one could blame me for wondering after last time.'

'Oh that.' Tamsin grinned. 'Don't worry, all parents and guardians were informed and asked to make suitable arrangements, but I didn't need that from Felix. I knew I could get home. On my own.'

Liz made no comment to this proud boast, but the expression on her face was of deep concern as if she thought that Tamsin was making all this up. But that was her problem, Tamsin thought as she watched the older woman return to her place behind the counter. And how was anyone supposed to know that Felix wasn't at home and couldn't be reached for a while? Where was he anyway when he was needed?

She picked up her glass and sipped thoughtfully. She had got this far on her own anyway. Liz whom she had to admit had always been there for her, ever since she was little and Felix could think only of his pots and the setting up of his gallery. His daughter had always come a close second. She had known that for years.

Now, seated at a table out of sight of most of the customers, she was mature enough to understand the worry she must have been to him, always needing to be looked after when he was struggling to get things going. She could see him now with that slightly vulnerable look he had when something seemed to be defeating him and then the sudden lighting up of his face before he lunged at her and held her close. His soothing words of comfort had been for himself as much as for the little girl so close to his heart. She could see that now, quite clearly, and felt ashamed.

She swallowed the rest of her drink in a couple of angry gulps. Last time she hadn't had the sense to phone Felix instead of taking off from school in a panic and look where it had got her. Luck had been with her then. Luck that the woman who had found her half-dead at the gate had the sense to drive her straight back to school, no questions asked. Well, not many. Not that she had been missed anyway until she turned up again and then faces had been decidedly red and serve them all right.

There was a bustle at the door as two customers tried to get out at the same time as someone was coming in.

'Felix!' Tamsin sprang up, nearly knocking over her empty glass in her haste to reach him.

'Tamsin.' His face broke into a grin and he lifted her off the ground in a tight hug.

'Oh, Felix.' She was so pleased he was here that tears welled in her eyes.

'So where's your luggage?' he asked as he set her down again.

Tamsin glanced at her rucksack by the wall. 'Travelling light?'

'Not you. Come on, where is it?'

'Back at the station being looked after. It'll be OK.'

He frowned. 'You're too casual, Tamsin. One day you'll be in trouble, left stranded somewhere with your belongings stolen. And what will you do then?' Felix raised an eyebrow.

She smiled. 'Dear Felix. You sound as if you cared.'

'I'll settle with Liz and then we'll be off to collect your stuff.'

'But that defeats my purpose,' she objected. 'I wanted to do the whole trip home without bothering anyone.'

'Least of all me?'

'You could say that.'

'I've let you down again, haven't I, Tamsin,

81

not being where I was supposed to be?'

He looked so downcast that her heart softened.

*　　*　　*

Crag Cottage, when they got there at last, surprised her with its unfamiliar tidiness. No piles of old newspapers, abandoned crockery and cushions on the dusty floor anymore. Or jerseys slung across the backs of chairs and open suitcases left for the unwary to trip over.

'What's this?' she said.

He carried in her suitcase and prepared to take it upstairs. 'Thought it needed it,' he said, without looking at her.

'But why now? Are you expecting someone else?'

'Maybe, one day.'

'Felix! We never have visitors.'

He paused halfway up the staircase, balancing the suitcase on the step above. 'Doesn't mean to say we never will.'

'Who is she?'

The short silence before he spoke felt threatening. 'Someone I met,' he said quietly.

'That's no answer.'

'I invited her to come and see the studio. That's all.'

She knew it wasn't all but she didn't want to hear any more and wouldn't question him further.

He shrugged, turning his face away from her. 'It may not happen.'

'Hurry up with that suitcase. I want to get unpacked,' she said. The sooner she had strewn her own belongings about the place to stake her claim to her own territory the better for her peace of mind.

* * *

Next day, Shona waved off the minibus with a feeling of relief even though she normally enjoyed looking after the comfort of the guests. Who would have thought that Rex would be such a pain, seeming not to know the first thing about leading a walking group? But today it was all planned for him and he and the group had pored over the route she had suggested and seemed happy with it all.

As soon as they had gone, Jack called Shona into the office. Ingrid was there, too, and looked up with a frown.

Shona looked at her thoughtfully. Today Ingrid's flushed face and jerky movements were totally unlike her usual calm exterior. A guilty conscience about something?

'Ingrid's just off to the post office,' Jack said. 'We need to talk, Shona.'

She swallowed hard. 'Yes, Jack,' she said, her voice faint. He looked at her in concern. 'Nothing wrong, is there?'

To her relief his voice was causal, friendly

almost. Maybe she had nothing to fear after all. She managed to smile. 'I . . . I hope not.'

She heard Ingrid close the door behind her and at once the atmosphere lightened.

'Sit down,' Jack said.

She did so, smoothing her long skirt over her knees and trying not to feel guilty about something for which she was not to blame. She owed him an apology that was clear, but in justifying her actions she would have to land Ingrid in it. Maybe knowing that was the reason for Ingrid's strange manner.

Jack smiled, the lines round his eye crinkling. 'No need to look so downcast,' he said, swivelling round in his chair to reach inside a drawer of the desk. He pulled out a file and opened it. 'As you know we have the history group booked in the week after next and a watercolour course the week after that. Unfortunately the painting tutor is ill and has to pull out. I want you to run through the list of tutors here and see if any are available.'

'But how will I know if they're any good?'

'They will be. We only have the best and these are all tried and tested. The short notice might be a problem, but do your best.'

'And if I can't find a replacement?'

'We cancel the course. We don't want that if we can avoid it. Bad for business.' He replaced the list in the file and handed it to her.

She nodded as she took it from him.

'Make it your first priority.'

'Of course.'

'I'm off for a day or two so I'll have another little job for you but we'll go into that at lunch.' His sudden smile had her smiling too. 'Ingrid's got a lot on her plate at the moment. I'm getting the small room next door fitted up for your office use as soon as we can to give you some privacy. Ingrid's been on to the local builder who says he can fit the work in between bigger jobs.'

'That sounds good,' Shona said as she got up. 'I'll get on to the tutor problem straight away.'

'Use the phone in the kitchen for the time being,' he said.

Mags was rolling out pasty on the wooden table, her cheeks flushed and her eyes bright. Shona smiled at her obvious enjoyment as she wielded the large wooden rolling pin as if it had done her an injury.

'Apple pie,' Mags said. 'Jack's favourite.'

'I've got a job to do for him,' said Shona. 'I've been told to use the phone here.'

'Help yourself,' said Mags. 'I'll make coffee when I'm done here,' said Mags firmly as she placed a sheet of pastry over a large enamel plate. She lifted it up and pricked up a knife to trim the edges.

'You look expert at that,' said Shona.

'Years of practice.'

'I suppose. Mags, do you know anything about the tutors that come here?'

'Me?'

'I've got to find a replacement for one for the week after next. Watercolour.'

'Ingrid's the one to ask about that.'

'She's gone off to the post office.'

Mags frowned. 'She didn't tell me. I've letters to go and Donald left in the minibus before they were ready. He'll do some business for Jack in Dumfries and back to the Forest Park to pick the group up at four o'clock.'

'I'll take your letters when I've made some calls,' said Shona as she reached for the phone on the wall. She ran her finger down the list. No answer to the first number she tried, or the second. The third sounded hopeful but would get back to her this evening. She explained that she needed to know at once but would phone again if she hadn't found anyone.

'Is one of them Mervyn Howard from Edinburgh?' Mags asked as she spooned apple on to the pastry. 'Try him. Ingrid likes him. He might do.'

Shona smiled as she dialled the number, trying to imagine someone that Ingrid liked. Tall, dark and handsome? Quite likely. No, on second thought, medium height would be better and a liking for the same rather way-out clothes that Ingrid favoured. Flowing and artistic-looking. But whatever he looked like he sounded pleasant enough when he answered and was agreeable to standing in at short notice.

86

She replaced the receiver with a feeling of a job well done and was glad to sit at the table while Mags made the promised coffee. Afterwards she walked down to the end of the drive with Mags' letters in her hand.

*   *   *

Shona joined Jack for lunch in the dining room and while they ate the sandwiches and salad Mags had prepared he told her of the Orchid Fair in Cheshire he was planning to visit. 'I'll be away for about three days,' he said. 'It's an important event.'

She nodded. 'An annual one?'

'It will be from now on. I'm hoping to pick up something really special. I'd like you, Shona, to keep an eye on my beauties while I'm gone as Ingrid's busy. Will you do that?'

'Of course.'

'Only a couple need frequent watering. The rest will cope till I get back. Ingrid has typed a list of instructions out for you so there's no problem. You'll find it in the folder. Thanks for sorting the new tutor.'

Mags brought in the apple pie and set it in front of Shona for her to serve.

The golden crust was crisp and sweetly-scented steam rose as Shona cut into it, making her eyes water.

'This looks good,' said Jack, taking his serving from her. She handed him the jug of cream.

He was good company when he was relaxed. She wondered if she was wise to raise the subject of not being here on duty the other evening or whether it was better to say nothing. She hated this feeling that she was in the wrong and longed to have things straight between them.

He raised his glass to his lips. 'Something troubling you, Shona?'

She shook her head. 'Not really. A bit of a responsibility looking after the orchids, that's all.'

'You'll cope.' He sounded so full of confidence in her that she felt a warm flush in her cheeks. She would do everything in her power to make sure his trust was well founded in spite of Ingrid's attempts to undermine her.

A sudden thought struck her. 'You said there were two orchids that needed frequent watering, Jack. Which are they?'

He looked amused as he wiped his lips with his napkin. 'There's my new baby in its own hanging basket in the east window of the conservatory. Do you know the one I mean? It's labelled, of course, as they all are. *Coelogyne cristata* would you believe, a long name for such a pretty little white frilly one. *String Of Pearls* to you and me. She needs to be watered liberally at the moment, but don't let her sit in water as that could rot her tender shoots.'

'And the other?'

'*Dendrobuim* or *Sailor Boy*. The same goes for him. Water from the top and allow to drain thoroughly. Anyway, good luck.' He got up, preparing to leave.

She smiled as she stood up too. 'With all your written instructions I should be all right.'

His eyes lit up as he smiled. 'Good girl. I'm going off this afternoon, by the way.'

SHONA SEES MORE OF FELIX

'We're lost,' said Rex, a hopeless tone in his voice that sent shivers down Shona's spine as she stood among the orchids in the conservatory.

'How can you be lost?' she cried. 'Why weren't you following the route we planned?'

'It's all trees round here and we can't see anything,' he wailed. 'Someone went off ahead. When we caught up with him the path ran out and we can't find the way back.'

This was ridiculous. 'You've still got your leaflet of the walk with you?' she asked. 'Can't you see where you are on that?'

'You'll have to get someone out to find us,' he gasped out.

Shona felt a moment's panic as she visualised the extent of the area. 'Listen, Rex. How far had you walked when you left the route?'

He hesitated and she heard the rustle of paper. 'Three miles, I think.'

'Did you head off left or right?'

'My battery's running out.'

Too late. Rex had gone. Incredible to think that a party of adults couldn't suss out where they were between them. Now what was she to do?

For a moment she stood motionless, aware of the sweet smell from the special orchid nearby and the rustle of foliage against the glass roof from the movement of air from the open door. She had thought looking after the two special plants might be a problem. But that was nothing to this.

Half closing her eyes in an effort to concentrate fully on the problem she remembered that the spare leaflets of the route were in a pile on the hall table.

The route was set out so clearly that even Rex shouldn't have had any trouble, she thought, gazing down at the open leaflet on the hall table before her. At the latest the group would have set off from the starting point before noon and it was now three o'clock. They had covered three miles, Rex said. But he might be wrong about that. She ran her finger along the route until she reached the three-mile point.

What was Rex doing letting one of the group wander off from the rest? A spurt of anger made her shiver. He was trouble enough when he was here at Ferniehope Castle, but even worse when let alone off into the unknown. Surely someone among the group had a phone with money on it?

She longed to jump in her car and go after them but leaving her post here with Jack away was definitely out of the question. And how likely was she to locate them on her own anyway? They could be anywhere in that vast expanse of trees and moor land.

An icy chill ran through her. The trouble for Jack would be huge once the Press got hold of the story. She could see the headlines now . . . GROUP FROM FERNIEHOPE CASTLE LOST IN FOREST. Or worse.

But what to do for the best? She was on her own in this and she had to cope. Jack had given Ingrid the afternoon off and Mags had gone off home to her cottage for a rest before starting the evening meal. Feeling helpless, Shona wandered into the office to see if by any chance there were instructions anywhere about what to do in any emergency like this. She found nothing.

She opened the brown folder in search of inspiration. The orchid instruction list was on top and other things Jack kept here such as the accommodation lists she had already seen and the one of suitable tutors to be called on when needed. She looked at the contents in despair and then noticed something that had

91

escaped her attention before. Under *Pottery and Ceramics* was Felix's name and mobile number.

She stared at it in surprise. Then on impulse she pulled out her phone and dialled.

He answered at once, his voice sounding so reassuringly close that tears sprang to her eyes on hearing his friendly voice.

He listened in silence as she poured out her worry and concern and then gave a grunt. As if he were deep in thought. 'Presumably they're the group I met when they first arrived at the castle?' he said. 'The leader's a short chap with a high opinion of himself?'

'Rex didn't sound as jaunty as usual a moment or two ago,' she said.

He laughed. 'Never fear. You're in luck. Your knight in shining armour will leap into action. We're near where they started out at this very moment, can you believe? Just stopped the car at the side of the road at the ringing tone. Rex and his merry crew will be on that minibus and no harm done.'

She had to believe him although she couldn't think how he could be as confident as he sounded. The planned route was among trees, obscuring distant vision. The only hope was that the group was moving slowly with long stops to examine their leaflets. Felix could cover the ground with speed, calling as he went. He would ask people, too, who would tell him if they had seen a bewildered group seeking help.

* * *

The relief was enormous when at last she heard the crunch of gravel beneath tyres.

She opened the door and rushed to greet them.

They poured out of the minibus, laughing and talking, one or two staggering with pretended exhaustion when they saw her. 'Did you have a good day?' she asked.

'Brilliant,' the youngest member of the party said, grinning. 'Ask Rex.'

'I'll do just that,' she said with feeling. He had it coming to him for the worry he had caused.

He was the last out, waving to her as to a long-lost friend. 'No problem after all,' he called cheerfully.

She stared at him, unable to speak for a long shaking moment.

The rest of the group dispersed and the minibus drove off. She was reminded suddenly of the day she had first visited Ferniehope Castle and her confrontation with Jack. Then she had felt humiliatingly in the wrong. She wished Jack were here now to deal with the situation and prevent her venting her anger on the infuriating man in front of her.

'How did Felix find you?' she managed to get out as she struggled with her composure.

93

'We weren't lost,' Rex said. 'It was all a mistake.'

'Mistake?'

He looked at her curiously. 'The chap we met was quite useful to us, I will admit.'

'Good.' She clenched and unclenched her hands.

'He wanted the girl to come back in the minibus with us but she wasn't keen. She looked as if she wanted to be with him alone in that old van. I don't blame her, a good-looking chap like that. Anyone would.' He looked downcast for a moment, but then brightened. 'Anyway all's well that ends well.'

Shona knew suddenly that ranting at him would do no good at all since Rex was totally unable to see any point of view but his own. At least they were back safe and sound and hard as it was, she must leave it at that. She took a deep calming breath.

'Thanks for arranging the day out,' Rex said gently, taking her by surprise. 'You did well.'

She managed to smile at what seemed like an apology. 'I'm glad it went well for you, Rex.'

Her irony was lost on him, of course, but it felt good to say it. Only two more days of his visit was left, thank goodness. One thing was certain. She would make quite sure that tomorrow's programme for the group was so simple that even a five-year-old child could cope.

*   *   *

She owed Felix her heart-felt thanks and as soon as dinner was over she phoned him. 'When are you coming to inspect my studio?' he said when she had finished saying how grateful she was for his help.

'I'm on duty here for the next day or two.' She sighed with disappointment.

'Can't you just sneak away when he's not looking?'

'Sorry, Felix. You know I'd love to come.'

'Then I'll come to Ferniehope Castle to see you instead.'

'You will?' her heart lifted.

'Complete with daughter. A good excuse to get my foot back in the door. You know Tamsin's school's got a measle epidemic. So expect us in the morning sometime after breakfast.'

'That'll be great,' she said warmth flooding through her. 'I'll look forward to that.'

'Oh and Shona, d'you want some help with that ineffectual chap and his group? I'll come prepared with an idea or two to put before you, if you want. Just say the word.'

*   *   *

'Here we are at last,' said Felix, unfolding himself from the battered blue van he had parked at the bottom of the steps leading up to

95

the main door. Shona, glad that Jack wasn't here to see, ran lightly down to greet him as Tamsin emerged from the passenger seat. Her light skirt was so skimpy it almost wasn't there and she looked cold as she rubbed her bare arms as she stood looking about her. The girl made no attempt to follow them inside and as Felix didn't seem to mind Shona left her to her own devices.

'I've been stalling with the plans for today until you came,' she told him as they went into the hall. 'Everyone's in the lounge examining all the brochures and leaflets we have and trying to convince Rex that someone else should make the decision for them all.'

'That's me,' said Felix, grinning at her.

She liked the way he seemed totally at home here as if nothing could faze him. 'You seem confident that Rex will be willing for you to take the lead,' she said.

'Trust me.'

She smiled. 'It's good to have you here,' she said.

He seemed taller today in his dark sweatshirt with his rucksack slung over one shoulder. He was wearing shorts, long knee socks and bulky walking boots he made no move to take off.

'They're clean enough,' he said as he saw her looking at them. 'I wish you'd come with us today, Shona. Even Jack Cullen's not that much of a taskmaster, is he? Come on, live dangerously for once.'

'And lose my job?'

There was a movement behind her and she saw that Ingrid had come to join them. Her dark hair was pulled severely back from her face in a new style for her and she had on a loosely-fitting dress in garish colours Shona hadn't seen her wear before.

Surprised, she moved to one side. 'Was there something?' she asked.

'Why should there be?' said Ingrid in her hoarse voice, smiling at Felix.

He looked back at her for a moment, a stillness in his manner. Then, ignoring her, he pulled an Ordnance Survey map from his pocket and opened it.

'Shona, I'm surprised you haven't offered our guest hot chocolate,' said Ingrid in a teasing tone so unlike her normal one that Shona felt embarrassed.

'Not now, Ingrid,' Felix said impatiently.

Ingrid's smile faded and glancing from one to the other she returned to the office, her back rigid.

Shona hesitated, half-inclined to go after her. But what could she say? Ingrid's reaction hinted of trouble to come and she was sorry. She imagined her in the kitchen now pouring out her hurt to her mother. But how likely was that? Ingrid would be far more likely in the office pounding the computer keys.

Felix, seeming unaware of any

unpleasantness, was still studying the map. He looked round for somewhere to spread it and then chose the floor. He knelt down to examine it with his long hair falling forward. The soles of his boots looked worn and well scrubbed.

'So, what are your suggestions?' Shona asked, leaning over to look at the map too.

'Just one,' he said, pointing. 'Donald to drop us here at Leckie Shore. Can you see? There's a pleasant flat walk round the estuary and they can't go wrong with me to lead them. What do you say to that? There's plenty of interest to see there with the wildlife and so on and no one will get lost. Packed lunches?'

'All done,' she said.

He pointed to another spot on the map. 'Afterward we'll continue here to Marpethowe and Donald can pick the group up there in the minibus at an arranged time. What do you think?'

'Brilliant,' she said. 'What's at Marpethowe?'

'My studio.' He got to his feet and folded the map.

'And you'd show them that?'

'Why not? And my showroom too. Tamsin's been helping me get it ready for the coming season. There's plenty to look at and to buy if they feel inclined.'

'I see.'

'Any problem with that?'

'It sounds good,' she said. She wasn't sure that Jack would approve if he knew about the commercial angle, but Felix's plans sounded excellent in the circumstances. Rex and the group wouldn't get lost and hopefully would have a great day out into the bargain. Who was she to object?

A PIECE OF THE PAST RETURNS

Tamsin emerged from the side of the house as the minibus drove off. 'I thought you'd gone with them,' Shona said in surprise.

Tamsin shrugged her thin shoulders and looked so forlorn standing there in her scanty clothes that Shona felt a rush of compassion for her.

'Come inside and let's have some hot drinks to set us up,' she said, moving towards the open door.

Tamsin looked at her suspiciously. 'Set us up for what?'

'I'll be glad of your company, Tamsin.'

'Why?'

'Why not?'

Shona would like to have said that she was sorry for her, that she was uneasy about what Ingrid would do next, that she needed some company to take her mind off Rex and his group. She couldn't help dwelling on where

Felix was taking them today, either. Leckie Shore was the place she most wanted to be with him and she resented him being there with others. How selfish was that?

Aware that Tamsin wouldn't want to hear these things she kept silent.

'I'm cold,' Tamsin said suddenly.

In the kitchen Mags tut-tutted when she saw them. 'You look half-starved, lassie,' she said, moving the kettle on to the hot plate of the stove where it immediately came to life, bubbling away joyfully. 'Didn't you bring anything warmer with you?'

'In the van,' said Tamsin, shrugging.

'Silly lass. What's it to be, hot chocolate like your father?' Tamsin shuddered as she hooked out a chair with her foot and plonked herself down at the table. 'No way. Tea please.'

'Me too,' said Shona. 'I'll be back in a minute.'

When she returned with the brown folder they were both at the table, the large brown tea pot between them. Mags poured a third cup and passed it to Shona. Already Tamsin was looking less pinched.

'Jack's asked me to look after his orchids,' Shona said. 'I've got the instructions Ingrid typed out for me. Would you like to give me a hand, Tamsin?'

'She's going to keep you hard at it today then,' said Mags, a broad smile creasing her pleasant face.

'Better than tramping about the countryside with that boring lot,' said Tamsin.

Shona relaxed a little as she drank her tea. Tamsin's words sounded bitter but the girl was smiling too.

'I'll do us a nice lunch,' Mags promised.

'Spaghetti Bolognese?'

'Do you still not get that in that fancy school of yours?'

'It'll always be my favourite,' said Tamsin, staring dreamily into her empty cup.

Shona, watching her, thought how pretty she looked when she let herself loosen up.

'Come upstairs with me and I'll lend you something warm,' she said. 'The orchids can wait for five minutes.'

'Wow,' said Tamsin as Shona unlocked her door and stood aside for Tamsin to enter before her.

'Nice, isn't it?' said Shona.

'Nice? What kind of word's that?'

'Splendid then,' said Shona laughing. 'Marvellous, wonderful.'

'Fabulous, impressive, superb,' said Tamsin dancing into the centre of the room and doing a twirl.

Shona found a navy sweatshirt for Tamsin and the girl put it on, still in raptures about the two rooms.

'I know I'm lucky,' said Shona as they went downstairs again.

Tamsin's face clouded. 'You should see our

101

place. Felix is always saying it needs a lick of paint but he doesn't do anything about it.'

'Why don't you have a go?'

'No way. I've a feeling it won't be my home much longer, not like it's been before.'

She sounded sad and Shona didn't want to pry. One day she might see for herself.

*   *   *

'But this isn't the frilly-leafed one like you said,' Tamsin objected.

'It isn't? Are you sure?'

Tamsin stood on one foot and leaned far forward to peer at the orchid in its pot hanging from the glass roof of the conservatory. Poised there, she looked like a ballet dancer on long thin legs.

'Mind you don't fall,' Shona warned.

Tamsin spun round, both feet on the ground now. 'You've got it wrong.'

Shona looking, reached forward and extracted the label from the pot. *'Pleione formosana,'* she read in bewilderment. 'This wasn't in this position the other day.' She replaced the label and ran her finger down the list until she came to the name. 'Direct light. Water freely,' she read out.

'I'll fill the small can,' said Tamsin.

'Not so fast,' said Shona. 'They don't all need watering. Give me a chance to check.'

Tamsin was peering at the labels of the

102

orchids on the windowsills now, exclaiming at the beauty of an orange one in full flower. 'This one's pretty,' she said. 'What a shame they're not all in bloom.'

Shona frowned as she picked up the green demister can from a shelf near the doorway. 'I know that one of them has to be misted with this thing every morning but where is it?'

'What's it like?'

Shona remembered the Latin name suddenly, the only one she could remember because both words began with the letter C and Jack had made a joke about it. 'It's a pretty white one . . . I've found it on the list. *Coelogne cristata. Likes full sunlight,* it says here. Soak the roots in water every other day. But that's not what Jack said.'

'So someone's got it wrong?'

'Not Jack,' said Shona. 'He showed it to me when it was hanging up. It's one he likes best. He told me its common name, a pretty one. I can't remember what it is at the moment.'

'So whose fault is it then?' Tamsin said, looking at her expectantly.

'I'll have to check this,' said Shona.

'So where's that woman, the secretary?'

'Ingrid. You don't think . . ?'

'Who else?' said Tamsin, her eyes alight with interest. 'You said she left the list for you.'

'Stay here,' said Shona. 'I'll find her.'

'I'm not going to miss this,' said Tamsin.

The office was empty. Shona checked the

103

other rooms and then pushed open the kitchen door to ask Mags if she had seen her.

'Gone to the post office,' came Mags' voice from the walk-in larder. She emerged with a string bag of carrots which she dumped on the draining board. 'There's a job here for you, young Tamsin, if you want one,' she said.

Tamsin grinned at her. 'No way. We've a mystery to solve. More interesting than carrots.'

'Be off with you then,' said Mags, no way put out.

'Come on,' said Tamsin, darting out of the kitchen and making for the office. 'We've got to do something quick. Which computer's hers?'

'Oh no, you can't . . .'

'Just watch me,' said Tamsin, sounding jubilant.

'What are you doing?' said Shona in alarm as Tamsin strode over to Ingrid's laptop.

'Investigating, of course,' said Tamsin, peering forward as Google came up on the screen and she typed in the words she wanted. 'Tell me the spelling of the one we want. Coe something.'

Shona did so, her throat dry with her dread of Ingrid's untimely return.

'We'll print this out now,' said Tamsin. 'I've got all the info we need for this little chap. The right info of course.'

The printer came to life and Shona

marvelled of the girl's knowledge and self-possession. Sitting there with her slim hands on the keys of a strange laptop she seemed perfectly in command of it all and much older than her fifteen years.

'Now we need a print-out of that list she gave you,' said Tamsin. 'Wait a minute and I'll find it.'

A few moments later they had two of them, a copy of the instruction list in the folder and another, the correct one, as well.

'OK?' said Tamsin as she handed them to Shona. 'We've got all we need. Got a spare memory stick? I'd better back it all up.' Shona passed her one.

'Thanks. Now we'd better get out of here before the dragon returns.'

Back in the conservatory again Shona let out a huge breath of relief. Tamsin took the three sheets of paper and handed back the one with the information from the internet. She sat down on the stool and with her tawny head bent, compared the two lists of instructions.

'Ingrid's sure got it in for you too,' she said.

For a moment Shona failed to pick up on the implication. Then it sank in. 'You mean she doesn't like you, either?' she said.

'Like I care,' said Tamsin.

'But why not?'

'I'm not talking about it. I want to get to the bottom of this. Here, take the lists. You know more about orchids than I do.'

Shona sat down on the stool to study them. 'Look what she's done,' she said. 'She's moved the instructions for the orchids one place down. Now it makes sense.'

'So that's her trick. They've all got the wrong information so you'll water the wrong ones and leave the wrong ones dry. But we've got the proof we need to get her. She can't argue with this. Show this to Jack and she's finished.'

Shona got up slowly. 'Not so fast. The orchids come first.'

'Then Ingrid.'

'I'm so grateful to you,' said Shona, still feeling weak at the knees at the thought of what she might have done to Jack's precious orchids. His reaction would have been horrendous.

Tamsin looked determined. 'You've got to get Ingrid for this,' Tamsin said. 'It's not fair. If you don't get her I will.'

*   *   *

'And did you?' asked Liz with interest. Shona shook her head. They were seated side by side on the swing seat on the grassy mound at the back of Ferniehope Castle on Saturday evening. Rex and his group had left for home soon after breakfast and she had spent the intervening time supervising the cleaners as they prepared the rooms for the next influx

106

arriving on Monday. Now she could relax in Liz's company.

'I haven't seen Ingrid since,' she said.

'Lying low?'

'Seems like it. Thanks for coming, Liz. I needed to talk.'

'It was a perfect evening for a walk.' As Liz leaned back in a reclining chair, a waft of flowery perfume floated in the calm air.

Shona gazed across the shadow-rippled grass to the bed of early tulips near the wall, highlighting the rough stone. 'Jack would have blown his top if I'd killed off any of his precious orchids. Tamsin saved my life.'

'Tamsin's a good child with a head on her shoulders,' said Liz, rocking gently.

'I'd do anything for that girl at the moment. Mind you, I had to leave the place unattended while I drove her home. I had my heart in my mouth, I can tell you, in case a crisis occurred while I was away.'

'What did Felix say when you showed up?'

Shona frowned. 'Nothing. He wasn't there. I just left her and got back. She said she's used to it.'

Liz laughed, smoothing down her pink fluffy cardigan over her ruffled blouse. 'I feel sorry for her with that father of hers always off on some mission or other.'

'Felix has been helpful to me too,' said Shona. 'He suggested a good trip out for the clients yesterday, sightseeing and shopping. It took a load off my mind. And now they've gone.'

'And Jack's not back yet?'

'Home tomorrow.'

'And will you tell him what happened with the orchids?'

'I'll confront Ingrid first.'

'Good luck.'

Shona gave a little shiver though the evening air was mild. 'Tamsin made me promise to hide the brown folder away so Ingrid can't replace the instruction list with the right one.'

'Her father's made a good job of bringing Tamsin up for all his erratic ways. He used to work here, you know. Ran a ceramics workshop, but of course it didn't last what with him being so resentful of Jack.'

'He was? But why?'

'You know Felix's aunt once owned the castle?'

Shona leaned forward. 'She did?'

'Her will was complicated and Felix was left only part owner of Ferniehope and so it had to be sold. Jack could see the potential of the place even though it was in a dilapidated state when Miss Agnes Langholme died and needed thousands spent on it.'

'Aunt Aggie!' said Shona in amazement.

'You knew her?'

'Felix used to talk about her when we were young. So Rich Aunt Aggie really existed?'

Shona leaned back in her chair. Just wait till she told Jodie when she phoned her this evening!

'They were close, Felix and his aunt,' said Liz, shifting a little in her seat. 'It's hard for him knowing that the castle is no longer in the family. He grew up here, you know.'

Shona looked thoughtfully at the castle building, in shadow now as the sun sank behind the trees.

'He must have loved it so,' she said, a lump in her throat. 'What must Felix have felt like watching Jack Cullen pour money into the place to change it from a family home to a smart conference centre for strangers?'

Liz gave a deep sigh. 'Och well, that's the way things go. Always change and moving on. And so must I. It's getting late.' She struggled out of her chair, buttoning her cardigan to the neck. 'It's been a grand evening for a talk, Shona, and I'll be thinking of you tomorrow and your fight with Ingrid.'

'Fight's a good word,' said Shona, laughing. 'And Ingrid's not going to win this one.'

'TELL ANYONE AND YOU'RE DEAD.'

Shona took a quick look at the orchids before breakfast next day to check that all was in order and then joined Mags in the kitchen.

The rich scent of roasting meat made her nose twitch. 'What is it today, Mags?' she asked, slipping into a seat at the breakfast table.

Mags, peeling potatoes at the sink smiled broadly. 'Roast pork,' she said. 'Jack'll want lunch early, I expect. He always does when he comes home on a Sunday morning. Scrambled eggs and mushrooms on toast do you?'

'My favourite,' said Shona.

She began to eat, her mind filled with the imminent confrontation with Ingrid. Yesterday her anger had made it seem easy, but in the light of day she was dreading it.

The hall door slammed. Ingrid? Putting down her knife and fork, Shona leapt up. Now for it! Heart thudding, she walked out of the kitchen, her head held high.

*   *   *

Jack Cullen backed his car into his usual parking space, got out and stretched. Being back at Ferniehope Castle felt as good as always and he took a deep breath of air that seemed to have the elixir of life in it. A few months ago leaving his clients would have been unthought-of, but now with Shona in attendance he had no worries. A great girl, Shona. Harley de Los had thought the world of her abilities. His luck was in when Harley left for the States and Shona needed other

110

employment.

He smiled as he clicked the car doors shut, anticipating Mags' huge smile of welcome when she saw he was home safe and sound. He'd had a good trip away at the orchid fair even though he'd spent more than he intended. But how could he help that when there was so much on offer?

Leaving his kit in the car to be unloaded later, he crossed the gravel to the back door and entered the kitchen on a breath of breezy air.

'Hi there, Mags, how's it going?' He sniffed in appreciation. 'Something smells good.'

She turned away from the sink and looked him up and down, smiling broadly. 'No need to ask how you got on at that flower place. You look blooming.'

He laughed at the unintended pun. 'It was great. A lot of exotic beauties new to me and I'm afraid I couldn't resist. I'm expecting a delivery in the next day or two.'

Mags tut-tutted her disapproval. 'Wasting good money when you've got so many of them already. What's the sense in that?'

'I've got no sense obviously, Mags.'

'You'll regret it one of these days.'

He laughed again. 'I'd better go and inspect my lovelies before I do anything else.'

'Shall I make coffee?' Mags dried her hands and reached for the kettle.

'Why not? Bring it into the conservatory,

111

will you? Shona and I have some catching up to do.'

As he went into the hall he heard raised voices. He didn't at first register that they were coming from his office. Then he paused in surprise, and before opening the door in time to see Shona, red-faced, staring at Ingrid whose words seemed to tumble over each other in her hurry to get them out of a mouth contorted with fury.

*   *   *

When Shona had reached the open office door five minutes earlier, Ingrid was hanging her dark jacket over the back of her computer chair. Was it imagination or did her shoulders have a triumphant look about them?

'One moment, Ingrid,' Shona said, her heart thudding.

Ingrid swung round, smiling. 'You want me? Has something happened?'

'Such as what?' Shona said, her voice rising at Ingrid's look of expectancy. 'Orchids dying because of wrong treatment and me to blame? What sort of mean trick is that?'

Ingrid opened her eyes wide. 'I can't think what you're talking about.'

'Believe me, you can.' With a flourish Shona opened the folder she had brought in with her and extracted the sheet of false instructions that Ingrid had typed out for her. 'How do you

112

explain this?'

The expression in Ingrid's eyes was triumphant. 'Tried it out, did you?'

Shona felt herself flush. 'Luckily, I'm not that stupid. You transposed the information for each orchid down one line.'

'Don't you dare to accuse me of anything?'

'There's no way you could have done this by mistake. This was a deliberate nasty trick to get me into trouble.'

'Says who?' Ingrid's laugh was harsh as she snatched the paper and tore it into shreds. 'So where's your proof now?' She dropped the pieces into the waste paper basket and then opened the lid of the laptop.

'It's no good wiping off the evidence now,' cried Shona. 'I've got more copies. And what's more it's all saved on memory stick.'

Ingrid glared at her. 'You have, have you?'

'I've got proof, Ingrid. Remember that, and if you think it's a threat, you're absolutely right.'

'Tell anyone and you're dead,' Ingrid hissed.

'So you admit it?'

'No way,' she cried as she lunged forward. 'Now get out.'

Alarmed, Shona took a step back.

The office door opened.

*   *   *

'Drink this,' Jack said, handing Shona a mug of

steaming coffee. He had taken one look at the two furious girls, caught hold of Shona and propelled her towards the conservatory. She had shown no resistance as he half-pushed her on to a low stool in the shade. 'Stay there,' he ordered, not even glancing at his orchids.

Ingrid had seen fit to disappear, for a cooling off session he hoped.

Shona looked stunned, he thought as he returned with the tray, as well she might after that fracas.

She put out a shaking hand to take the mug from him.

'No,' he said sharply. 'I'll do it. I need to know what's been going on.'

He placed her mug of coffee on the floor near where she was seated. 'Don't kick it over.'

'I . . . I'm sorry about all that,' she whispered.

He poured coffee for himself from the tray on the central bench. Holding both hands round the mug, he leaned against the door frame and looked at Shona closely. 'So Ingrid's temper got the better of her again?' he said. 'I should have warned you. She's good at her job and you have to learn to deal with it sooner rather than later.'

She gave a little gasp. 'But Ingrid went too far . . .'

He frowned. 'For your own good take on board what I've just said. I mean it, Shona. What's between the two of you must stay that way. I insist on it.'

He knew he was being harsh but there was no other way. Ingrid's bursts of temper were just that, sudden and soon over. He must give Shona credit for realising that now and standing well clear.

He sighed. 'I didn't expect this sort of welcome home after a fabulous few days at the orchid fair.' His euphoria had vanished now and the sight of Shona drooping on her stool filled him with concern so deep he was at a loss as how to handle it.

'Tell me about the last days of the rambling group,' he said. 'You coped with them?'

She raised her head. 'I needed help with that too,' she said. 'I planned a day's walking in the forest park. There should have been no trouble, but they got lost. I phoned someone and he helped out. He was in the area. He found them.'

Jack gave a scornful laugh. 'Their leader was totally inept. A black mark against his name in the book, please, for future reference. We won't have him here again. And the rest of their time?'

'Felix helped me there too. He came here prepared to take them over. He did a great job.'

'Felix Langholme!' Jack slammed his mug down so hard on the tray that coffee flew in all directions. 'I don't have that man at Ferniehope Castle, d'you understand? Surely

I'd made that clear already?'

Shona stared at him, white-faced. 'I don't believe this,' she said. 'There was a crisis. I care about those people. I liked arranging their day so they were happy. I couldn't just leave them there, worried probably about getting back. I had to do something.'

'But not that.'

Jack picked up his cup and took a gulp of coffee.

Furious, Shona lashed out at him. 'What was I supposed to do . . . alert the emergency services and make Ferniehope Castle a laughing stock when the media got hold of the story?'

'You had no right to involve Felix Langholme.'

'I had a choice about asking for his assistance and I made it,' said Shona. 'He came at once when I asked.'

'Isn't it enough that you went to meet him when you should have been deputising for me here? Oh yes, I know about that but decided to overlook it at the time. And now this.'

She raised her eyes to look at him and he knew that she dreaded what she should see in his face. 'That wasn't my fault. I understood that you had given permission. And the decision I made to involve Felix was the right one in the circumstances. And what's more his daughter, Tamsin, helped me with the orchids.'

116

He felt heat shoot into his face. 'His daughter? I don't believe it.' His fury was hard to control, but he managed with an effort. Expecting the worst, he looked about him at his healthy plants. He felt their well-being as if they had spoken to him, but for the first time ever they had no power to calm him.

'Tamsin was good,' said Shona, her voice defiant.

'That precocious child!' He breathed deeply.

'She's as helpful as her father and I was grateful.'

'You let her loose in here, touching my orchids?'

'I touched them. No one else.'

He stared at her for a long moment. Then he got up and strode from one orchid plant to the other, aware of Shona's gaze on his back that seemed to cut him with fire. He spun round. 'She's trouble, you'd be well advised to avoid her in the future.'

*   *   *

Sunshine shone through the trees now, touching Shona's side of the conservatory with delicious warmth. She watched Jack examining the white frilly orchid with tenderness at the same time listening to him railing against Felix for coming to Femiehope Castle to help her out of a difficulty that would have rebounded on the place if he hadn't.

He was an arrogant, ungrateful bully.

She thought of Felix coming to her aid, delighted to be of use to their clients even though he despised the owner of the conference centre for the wrong he had done him in the past. How unselfish was that? She thought of Tamsin's amazing ability to save her from deep trouble. She hadn't been permitted to voice her point of view as to what had been happening and how unfair was that? Why hadn't he wanted to get to the bottom of the verbal fight between Ingrid and herself?

Jack had stopped his perambulations now but the angry mask on his face hadn't slipped. 'Take the rest of the day off and keep out of Ingrid's way,' he ordered.

Shona got up, eager to escape to her room. With her back held straight she left him to it. He hadn't asked if all the arrangements were in place for the arrival of the new group arriving tomorrow.

She threw herself on her bed, wishing she had kept her cool in the face of Ingrid's provocation. That way she would have been more in command of the situation. But of course she had the upper hand anyway because she had the proof of Ingrid's felony. And Ingrid knew that.

Feeling slightly better, Shona sat up and grabbed Toby from her bedside table.

'Are we going to take this lying down?' she

118

demanded.

'No way,' she imagined him saying. 'We're a team, you and I. We'll show them!'

She replaced the toby jug on the table and picked up her mobile.

*   *   *

The island looked closer today because the intervening water was narrower than it had been the afternoon she had first revisited this spot. Was the tide on the way out or in . . . waxing or waning? Coming in, probably.

Shona stood on the empty beach, considering how long she would have to wait for the water to disappear and then picked up a pebble to add to the cairn of stones.

Overhead a lone seagull let out a mournful cry as it winged its way down the estuary and she wondered where its companions were on the sunny spring morning.

Since Liz was too busy to talk the next best thing was to be alone to think things out and come to terms with Jack's reaction. Several cars had been parked in the car park of Bessie's Kitchen as she drove past and she was glad for Liz's sake because she needed the custom. With luck there would be even more customers presently, arriving for a Sunday lunch that she knew would be excellent.

Just like Mags, Shona's mouth watered at the thought of that roasting pork filling the kitchen at Ferniehope Castle with its rich aroma.

But she wasn't really hungry. Standing here on this lonely shore with the rising breeze ruffling her hair she was reminded of those family holidays long ago and was shaken with such devastating sadness that she sank to the shingle and sat with her head resting on her knees. Dad had always been so quick to sympathise with her longing to reach the island. And now Dad was gone and suddenly her loss had hit her in this devastating way. Tears welled up and a huge lump filled her throat.

She had tried to make Dad's last years comfortable for him, but now she wished she could have brought him up here on holiday, staying perhaps at a farm nearby so that they could relive together some of the memories that meant so much to them. But Dad's arthritis prevented any long car journey.

She raised her head, tears streaming and saw Felix trudging along the coast path towards her, a rucksack on his back. Wiping her face to disguise the grief that had taken her unawares Shona struggled to her feet.

'Hey, what's this?' Felix called as he got close.

She gave a shaky laugh that turned into a sob.

At once his arms were round her and her face rubbing against the rough wool of his jersey. 'It's all right,' she murmured, pulling away at last. 'It's nothing.'

He held her at arms length and looked at her critically. 'Nothing, eh? You could have fooled me.'

'It's just that . . . I don't know why . . . my dad died a few weeks ago.'

'And it suddenly overcame you when you were least expecting it?'

She nodded, glad of his understanding. 'I suppose it's this place, Leckie Shore,' she said. 'He loved it so.'

'Didn't we all?' said Felix, shrugging his arms out of his rucksack and undoing it. 'I've a flask of coffee here and this is a fine moment for it. Agreed?'

She nodded again and watched him pour the coffee from his flask into two white beakers before handing one to her.

They drank in companionable silence, watching two dinghies being rigged for sailing. The red sails and orange buoyancy aids of the crews were bright splashes of bright colour against the grey surroundings as they moved across the hard sand to the water's edge.

'Your father was a fine man with the patience of a saint,' Felix said at last. 'I must have tried it a time or two. D'you remember those crazy pots I fashioned each time we walked across to the island?'

'What did you do with them?' said Shona. 'Do you suppose they're still there?'

'Stored in that secret camp place we made? We'll have to investigate over there one day, don't you think?'

She smiled, all traces of her tears gone. Being here with Felix was good. She hoped the threatened rain would hold off.

A sudden gust of wind filled the sails of the dinghies out there on the water.

Felix reached for her empty beaker. 'Another?'

'If there is some.'

He grinned at her, the lines round his eyes deepening. 'I wouldn't be offering if the flask was empty, now would I?'

'You are so thoughtful.'

'I aim to please.'

This time when they had finished he collected the beakers and replaced them in the rucksack, looking up into the sky as he did so. 'Fate,' he said. 'Meeting like this, Shona, don't you think? Rex and his merry group thought this was the best walk they'd ever done. Scenic and not too strenuous, you see.'

'So you hit the right note here for him,' said Shona. 'Maybe for others, too, who like to walk but are not serious walkers. There's a free time built in the programme for each group. Some of them might like to do this one for a bit of relief from their studies.'

'Fancy seeing a bit of it for yourself? You could call it research.'

'Try me,' Shona said as she sprang up.

JACK'S FEUD WITH FELIX
CONTINUES

Shona waited for Felix to sling the rucksack up on to his back. Then they set off together across the springy turf on a path that led through brambles and gorse bushes. The sweet scent from the yellow gorse flowers hung on the breezy air and in the distance the hills were grey against the lowering clouds.

'We'll head up by the Water of Leck towards Anderleck for a couple of miles to let you see the lie of the land,' he said. 'Plenty of wildlife on offer as you'll see.'

'Like that cormorant over there?'

Shona looked back at the island, remembering the times of long ago when the days were endless and the tide always seemed too far out to walk across. Not like today when it was still rolling in.

'Retracing our steps to pick up your car won't be a problem,' he said. 'Things always look different from the other direction.'

'So I'll make sure not to look back as we walk then, shall I?'

He grinned at her. 'You've got the idea.'

She smiled back, happy in his companionship.

The path narrowed as they reached the riverbank and they walked in single file, Felix in front. Every now and again he paused to check she was coping with ground that became increasingly rocky.

'It won't be like this for long,' he promised.

Soon it was grassy again and she could see the inland mountains sharp against the dark clouds. A stand of trees gave shelter here and the view across the river was enticing. There was a faint muddy smell that wasn't unpleasant.

They reached a grassy slope backed by an outcrop of rocks. Felix paused. 'This'll be a good place to eat my piece.' He laughed at her enquiring expression. 'My piece? Haven't heard that before? Or maybe you've forgotten. It's the food I brought with me for lunch. Plenty for you, too, so that's all right.'

'I didn't think of bringing anything,' she said.

'You hungry?'

'I am now.'

They sat on tussocks of dry grass with their feet hanging over the low drop to the river. Below them lichened rocks nestled in the sandy ground and a cormorant disappeared beneath the grey water to emerge some distance away.

'Where were you off to when we met?' Shona asked.

'I set out to walk the path up to Anderleck and then down the other side of the river to the shore again and then make a wide circuit home through the Banderloch Mountains. You often see wild goat up there.'

'Sounds dangerous.'

'Not if you're a brave hunk like me.'

'Slay them with your bare hands, do you?'

He grinned. 'If necessary. But rarely is.'

'What's Tamsin doing today?'

'Tamsin?' A fleeting look of surprise flickered in his eyes. 'Oh, Tamsin. She doesn't believe in moving one foot in front of the other if she can help it.'

'She was so friendly and helpful to me the other day.'

'I never thought she'd turn into a stroppy teenager,' he said, frowning.

'She's so bright and clever.'

'We can't be talking about the same girl.'

'I like her.'

'She needs someone to care, I suppose,' he said, sighing. 'We seem to have lost it, she and I. Her school doesn't seem to be the answer I hoped for, but I can't take her away now.'

He gazed broodingly across to the mountains, his shoulders hunched. His hair, longer at the back, was slightly uneven and she wished she could touch it. His vulnerability tore at her heart.

'You said she needs someone to care about her,' she said, hoping that her words didn't sound like a criticism.

'I feel totally frustrated sometimes.'

'I'll be her friend. I'll look out for her, Felix.

I won't let her down.' A surge of happiness ran through her. Her words, lightly spoken were a sacred promise because she had promised Felix.

He smiled, his face lighting up in a way she remembered. She longed to tell him that she not only cared about his daughter but about him too.

Silence hung between them for a long moment. Then he began to pack his food container into his rucksack, pushing it in hard. 'We've already drunk the coffee I'm afraid.'

She immediately felt guilty. 'I didn't know it was part of your lunch.'

'Not to worry. Your need was greatest then.' He raised his face. 'I feel rain on the wind. Maybe this is a good point to turn back. You need hiking boots for the terrain I'll be covering.'

She smiled, struggling to hide her disappointment. 'No need for you to accompany me,' she said. 'I can get myself back to my car on my own. I'm not stupid.'

He looked at her, smiling. 'Far from it.'

'I'll think of you tramping through the mountains in the pouring rain.'

'You do that,' he said, heaving on his rucksack. 'Sure you'll be OK?'

'Sure.'

'I don't think the rain will come to much.' He glanced at his watch and already seemed miles away. 'See you, then.'

He didn't mention her day off on Tuesday or his promise to show her his studio.

She watched him go striding off, a tall man with his huge rucksack bobbing on his back.

He came to an outcrop of rock and she could see him no more.

Back at her car she got the local map out of her glovebox to check how close they were to his cottage and studio and found that only a mile or two separated them from where she was now.

*   *   *

Later, stacking the dishwasher at Bessie's Kitchen, Shona realised that Felix hadn't told her what his daughter was doing today while he was off marching through the mountains.

'All right in here?' Liz asked, coming with another stack of dirty plates. 'It's good of you to help, Shona. Are you sure you wouldn't rather be back at the castle putting your feet up?'

Shona took the plates from her. 'After being warned away by Jack? No thanks.'

'Lucky for me then.' Liz rubbed her hand across her moist forehead and leaned against the unit for a short rest. 'I wanted a huge clientele, but not all descending at the same time.'

Shona laughed as she straightened up again. 'Your reputation for Sunday lunch has spread far and wide.'

'Och, don't think I'm not grateful, Shona, wearying work though it is. If it was like this every day I'll be needing to take on more staff.'

'I'll call in for a progress report on my next day off,' Shona promised.

'You've got the wildlife people coming tomorrow?'

'You make it sound so interesting.'

'Good luck, anyway. And now I must get on.'

Shona continued with the stacking, glad that she had called in on the off-chance that Liz could use her help. Returning too early to Ferniehope Castle was not an option and this was the perfect solution.

*   *   *

Later, lying on top of the pink and cream patchwork bedspread, Shona phoned Jodie. She tried to keep her voice light but Jodie sensed that something was wrong and asked in her forthright way to tell exactly what it was.

'I met Felix this morning at Leckie Shore,' Shona said. 'I went there because I had some time off. He just appeared.'

'And?'

'And what?'

'Don't tell me you didn't get it together at last?'

'Oh Jodie.' Shona broke off before her voice

shook.

'What's the matter with that man, I want to know?'

'It's you and Duncan and the twins I want to know about,' said Shona, taking a hold of herself. 'Come on, spill.'

'Oh, Shona,' Jodie said, excitement in her voice. 'Someone's contacted Duncan wanting to know if he'll help him set up a website. He'll pay him of course. He'll bring his laptop round here.'

'That's great,' said Shona. 'Good luck to him.'

'That's him now,' said Jodie. 'Speak to you soon.' She rang off.

Afterwards Shona lay for a while with her eyes closed, listening to the sound of distant mowing and thinking of Felix striding away from her without a backwards glance. There was something odd about it, some feeling that disturbed her.

Then, sighing, she swung her legs off the bed, deciding to have a shower before the evening meal.

*   *   *

Mags had left chicken salad for two and set the table in the kitchen. Ingrid's absence was a relief Shona hadn't looked for.

They talked of the arrangements for the people arriving tomorrow.

'The historical society are coming next and have booked for another week in the autumn as well,' Jack added with satisfaction, helping himself to a jacket potato. He went on to tell her some of the historical sites in the area they hadn't had the opportunity to visit last time.

After the meal Shona made coffee that they drank at the kitchen table. Then together they cleared the table and while Shona put the remains of the salad away in the fridge Jack filled the sink with hot water and added a generous amount of washing up liquid. 'We'll not use the dishwasher for this lot,' he said.

'I owe you an apology,' he said when he had finished, leaning back against the sink.

A feeling of relief flooded through Shona.

'I know Ingrid can be difficult,' he said.

She nodded. Yes, Ingrid was difficult. Mean and calculating too. 'You were unfair to me,' she said. 'There's something you should know about what happened between Ingrid and me. I need to explain, to tell you . . .'

'No good will come of explanations,' he said. He looked troubled. 'Let it go, Shona. There was no need to ban you from the place for the rest of the day, and I'm sorry for that.'

She nodded, accepting his apology. Perhaps he was right. No harm had come to his orchids after all. She would be vigilant in future.

'So where did you take yourself off to?'

'I spent time with friends,' she said.

He tapped his fingers on the unit behind

him, looking as if he wanted to question her further. She hadn't seen him so unsure of himself before.

He straightened. 'I see. Well, I won't keep you. We'll meet at breakfast.'

As she went up to her apartment she heard him go into the office and close the door firmly behind him.

*   *   *

Jack made no more mention of the bad feeling between herself and Ingrid in the days that followed except to tell her that Ingrid was planning on taking a few days off the following week.

'It's our least busy time now the bookings are all done,' he said. 'I'm sure you can cope in the office with any enquires and such like?'

'Of course,' she said, glad that she could look forward to a few Ingrid-free days.

She busied herself with the comfort of the new clients, finding everything much easier now because she had done it before. On her day off she went with them on the Kite Trail and enjoyed a fascinating day out. She returned to Ferniehope Castle exhausted but glowing with long hours in the open air, having learnt more about the birds that, reintroduced into the area, now soared above the forest parks again.

It wasn't until the following Sunday evening

she had the chance to visit Liz as she had promised.

Sunday lunch at Bessie's Kitchen had been as popular as ever and now that the sun was sinking in the sky Liz was relaxing on a wooden sun lounger on her patio at the back.

'Shona, you've come,' she said with pleasure, struggling to a sitting position.

'Don't get up,' said Shona pulling forward one of the wooden chairs. 'Didn't I say I would? Or did you expect Jack to lock me in my room on a diet of bread and water so I couldn't escape?'

Liz laughed, but there was a wary expression in her eyes. 'You never did tell me why you had reservations about me working there,' Shona said as she settled herself comfortably. 'Did I? I'd forgotten.'

'When I first called in here on the rainy afternoon. Don't you remember?'

'I suppose I was anxious about the feud Jack's got with Tamsin's father. It's local knowledge you see and I didn't know whether to tell you or not.'

'I see.'

'I don't know Jack well. I suppose I thought he might be a difficult man to work for.'

'He's a perfectionist,' said Shona, gazing out over the calm water of the estuary. 'Hardworking himself and expecting the same of his staff. And I can't believe he's dishonest.'

'Well no, perhaps not,' Liz conceded.

'Tamsin came in here yesterday. At a loose end I suppose.'

Shona frowned. 'I had no idea she was still at home. She said she was fine when I spoke to her on her mobile.'

'Something will have to be done about her before she lands herself in more trouble.'

'And I'll have to do it,' said Shona leaping up.

Liz pulled her fluffy cardigan round her more closely. 'What now?'

'I promised Felix I'd look out for her.'

'You'd interfere at this time of night?'

Shona dropped back on to her chair. 'I worry about her.'

'Felix will have to sort something out with the school. He may already have done so for all we know.'

'Of course,' said Shona. 'I over-reacted as usual.'

'You're a caring girl,' said Liz affectionately. 'Better to be like that than hard and selfish.'

Shona smiled. 'And you're a good friend to me, Liz. Now tell me how things are going with you.'

*　　　*　　　*

Shona drove back to Ferniehope Castle with much to think about. Should she take it upon herself to use the house phone at the cottage and ask about Tamsin and where she was? Or would Felix think she had taken too much on herself? He might well feel she was hounding him when it was none of her business.

But she had promised Felix she would look out for the girl.

She was still engrossed in the problem as she undressed later and slipped into bed.

Felix had confided in her about his frustrations in dealing with his daughter. She thought of his touching gratitude for her taking Tamsin back to school and his entertaining company at Bessie's Kitchen. Surely he would welcome her concern?

Afterwards they had gone out to the cars and he had greeted Toby as a friend. He considered a Toby jug a real person . . . amazing! But she did exactly the same thing too and this was a bond between them. The only bond? With pain she was beginning to think that it was.

Now she switched on the bedside lamp to reach for Toby, wanting to smooth the china of his ugly shape because Felix liked him.

He wasn't there.

She sat up and stared at the empty space where he should have been. Conscious of her beating heart, she lay down again. Had she taken him out with her this evening when she drove to Bessie's Kitchen? Perhaps needing him for company? Tired as she was after an exhausting day, she might well have done so and forgotten.

Midnight. Too late to check now.

No one knew that Toby lived on her bedside table. No one except Tamsin. Tamsin? But no, not for an instant could she think of Tamsin taking him. She was sure she could trust her implicitly. And yet . . . But definitely not.

Two important things to do first thing tomorrow then . . . check the car for Toby and phone Felix's cottage to enquire about Tamsin's welfare.

Falling asleep at last the two things merged in her dreams and she woke next morning unrefreshed.

A STARTLING REVELATION

At eight-thirty the next morning, a coach drove slowly up the drive to the castle, coming to a halt at the front of the building just as Mags carried the tray containing the teapot and coffee pot into the dining room.

'Listen!' said Jack, getting up from the breakfast table. Shona had heard the sound of tyres on gravel and the squeak of brakes too. 'They can't be here already,' she cried.

Jack, controlling his annoyance with obvious difficulty, strode to the front door.

His greeting was muted and Shona recognised the undercurrent of exasperation in his voice that the history group booked in for this week had ignored the request to time their arrival after eleven o'clock. Fortunately the rooms were all prepared. All that remained was for her to produce the list of rooms and all would be well.

Jack turned to her. 'They can unpack their luggage before they do anything else,' he said. 'The coach can then leave.'

This would mean an overcrowded entrance hall, Shona thought, but a glance at Jack's set face made her hesitate to suggest that room keys should be allocated first. People and luggage hustled round her.

The names on the list were blurred and running into each other in a way that made her dizzy. Then Toby's ugly features superimposed themselves. She gasped and let the paper fall. The noise round her grew in volume.

'What do we do now?' someone shouted. 'This isn't good enough.'

She heard Jack's sharp tones. 'One minute, please.'

The crowd parted to let him through. 'What's the matter, Shona? Can't you cope with something as simple as this?'

'Well yes, I . . .'

'Here, let me. I'll see you in the office. Wait there.'

Ashamed, she did as he said.

*   *   *

'So what was all that about?' he asked five minutes later. 'Early as they were, you should have been up to the job. What happened to you?'

'Toby's gone,' she said in desperation.

Jack's eyebrows shot up. 'Toby?'

Just before the coach arrived she had checked her car and was dismayed to find Toby was still missing and had gone in to breakfast. Jack, smart in his dark suit, white shirt and grey tie was already there. And then Mags carried the tray in and there was the bustle of people arriving.

'I left him on my bedside table and he's not there anymore. It sounds crazy . . .'

'Sure does. Explain, please.' He glanced at his watch. 'I'm due at the bank at nine-thirty.'

'My toby jug . . . I brought him with me. He's vanished.'

'Valuable?'

'To me.'

'You're not suggesting someone stole it?'

'But how can he be gone?'

'He couldn't have walked away on his own. You'd better make some enquiries. Mags might know something.' He looked at her closely and his voice softened. 'You're really upset about this, aren't you, Shona?'

His unexpected sympathy was nearly her undoing. She took a deep breath to stop herself dissolving into tears. 'He meant a lot to me.'

'Then do what you can,' he said, sounding businesslike once again. 'I'll see you when I get back. If there's been a theft I need to know about it. Do your best to cope with the arrivals, Shona. They've already eaten. Now they're unpacking. The leader knows you're in charge.'

The history group planned to visit Whithorn to see the finest collection of early Christian stones in Scotland. Free of responsibilities for an hour or so Shona returned to her apartment hoping that a miracle had happened and Toby was back in his usual place.

He wasn't, of course.

Sitting on her bed with her back turned to the empty space where he should have been she dialled Crag Cottage on her mobile.

The ringing tone stopped and a slurred voice muttered something.

'Tamsin?'

'Go away. It's too early.'

'Tamsin, is your father there?'

'Of course he's not. What do you want him for?'

'It's Shona here, Tamsin. I need to know. Are you all right?'

More muttering. 'I'm always all right.'

She didn't sound it.

'Tamsin, listen. I take it that Felix isn't there. Is he coming back soon?'

Silence. She was cut off. She tried Tamsin's

mobile but without success.

Frustrated, Shona went down to the office and tried the phone there with the same result.

She wasn't having a good day.

*   *   *

The track that led down to Crag Cottage was so rutted that Shona's car rocked from side to side even though the speedometer showed slower than walking pace. She should have left her vehicle at the top and walked down. Too late now.

And there was the cottage, picturesque in sunshine that trickled through the branches of an oak tree and made patterns on the grey roof. Nearby was a low wooden shack with a notice outside that told whoever was brave enough to negotiate the track that this was Langholme Studio and visitors were welcome.

Shona parked the car and a few moments later was knocking on the open door of the cottage. 'Anyone at home?' she called.

'Who's that?' came a suspicious voice from somewhere above.

'Tamsin?'

'Wait a minute. I'll be down.'

Encouraged, Shona went inside.

Tamsin joined her in the passage. 'Why are you here?'

'To see you, of course. You're here on your own. When will Felix be back?'

Tamsin shrugged her thin shoulders and opened a door that led into a back room. Shona followed.

'He thinks I'm going back to school,' Tamsin said.

'And you're not?'

'I'm sixteen now, aren't I?' Tamsin said defiantly.

'You've had a birthday? You mean . . . today?' Shona, horrified, looked about her at the signs of neglect in the dim room. No cards, no presents, no anything to show that the day was special.

For a moment she couldn't speak.

'Aren't you going to wish me a happy birthday?'

'I'll do more than that, Tamsin. You'll have the best day out I can manage.'

Tamsin looked down at her grubby T-shirt and ragged jeans.

'Then I'll have to change.'

While she was doing so Shona sat gingerly on an upright chair and thought hard.

A special lunch out somewhere, but where? Tamsin, in newer jeans and white T-shirt, was back before she decided.

'So where are you going? Ferniehope Castle?' she asked.

'Hardly.' Jack wouldn't approve of that, Shona thought with a shudder. In fact he wouldn't approve of what she was doing at all. But with luck he wouldn't be back for a while yet and Ingrid wasn't there to make trouble.

'You'll need some sort of jacket, Tamsin,' she said. 'We'll head west, shall we? See where we land up?'

'A mystery tour?' Settling herself in the passenger seat Tamsin looked cheerful.

*   *   *

Jack drummed his fingers on the table as he waited for Mags to come back into the kitchen from hanging a row of pristine-white tea towels on the line in the back yard to blow merrily in the wind. He had been back all of twenty minutes before he realised that Shona wasn't where he expected her to be. So where was she?

Mags' broad face flushed with pleasure to see him. 'I'll get some coffee on,' she said, dumping the empty clothesbasket on the draining board.

'Have you seen Shona?' he asked.

She looked surprised. 'Och no, not since breakfast.'

'Her car's not in the yard.'

Mags shook her head. 'So she'd gone out. Maybe an emergency somewhere?'

'She'd have told you, wouldn't she?'

Mags pursed her lips. 'Ingrid wouldn't have.'

'I need Shona to get some forms off since Ingrid's not here to do it.' He frowned. 'I'll

141

have to do it myself then. No coffee thanks, Mags.'

In the end he phoned Liz at Bessie's Kitchen. It was mid-afternoon now and he was seriously worried.

'Shona?' Liz's voice sounded relaxed. 'They were in earlier. Off somewhere for a day out they said. They didn't say where they were heading. Have you tried her mobile?'

'Several times. Out of range, I think, or the battery's down.'

'Sorry I can't be more helpful.'

'Not to worry. Thanks anyway.'

It wasn't until he'd replaced the receiver that he remembered he hadn't asked who Shona's companion was. He lifted the receiver again but then replaced it. What sort of a suspicious fool would he sound if he dialled Liz again to ask?

*   *   *

She couldn't dump Tamsin back at Crag Cottage knowing she was on her own, Shona thought as they sat eating ice-creams on the picnic bench overlooking the Leck River.

'Problems,' she said.

'What me?' said Tamsin, wiping her mouth with the back of her hand.

For the first time Shona wondered if she had done the right thing taking Tamsin off the way she had. Suppose Felix phoned the cottage

142

expecting his daughter to be there? Well, what if he did? Wasn't it his fault in the first place for going off somewhere on his own. But he wasn't on his own.

'You said "they" Tamsin. Who is Felix with?'

'Don't you know?'

'Should I?'

'That woman, of course, from your place.'

Shona stared at her. Ingrid had taken time off. 'You don't mean . . . ?'

Tamsin shrugged. 'Like I care.'

Shona felt herself turn cold and then hot with a huge flash of anger on Tamsin's behalf. 'Ingrid left yesterday morning. When did Felix leave?'

Tamsin shrugged. 'I don't want to talk about it.'

Shona didn't either. She knew in a sudden flash of self-knowledge that Tamsin's welfare was of prime importance at this moment. The shock of her discovery brought her to her feet. 'Come on!'

'Where are we going now?'

'How long will it take you to pack a bag?'

'Not long. Why?'

'I'm not leaving you on your own. You're coming with me.' She had done it now, well and truly.

*   *   *

143

The euphoria of her impulsive reaction had worn off by the time Shona parked her car at Ferniehope Castle. She went through the back entrance to the kitchen where Mags was peeling potatoes at the sink.

'So you've returned,' Mags said.

'I've taken Tamsin to stay with Liz for the night,' said Shona. 'I couldn't leave her alone in the cottage with her father away.'

Mags finished what she was doing and lifted the pan on to the cooker. Then she strained the potato peelings through the colander and emptied the contents into the bin she kept for the purpose.

'Felix thinks she's back at school,' said Shona.

Mags looked at her sternly. 'Expecting you to drive her back there, is she?'

'No way.'

Shona cleared her throat. 'I need to talk to Jack. Liz can only have her for one night. The room's booked after that.'

'So,' said Mags as if she hadn't spoken. 'You'd better tell me what's going on here. Her father's gone off. Ingrid too. There's been something in the wind for some time. Call it a mother's intuition. It's true maybe?'

'I'm sorry, Mags.'

'He's unpredictable and unthinking. But she'll cure him of that.'

'You don't mind about it?'

'It's that young lass I'm sorry for. Ingrid

144

won't want her, I know that.'

Shona looked at her gratefully. 'I thought I was the only one to care, Mags. Apart from Liz, of course.'

'And you want to bring Tamsin here?'

'Does Jack know about Ingrid?'

'I'm not the one to tell him.'

Shona sighed. 'So I will. I can't stand it, Mags. I'm in trouble enough already.'

'You are that,' Mags agreed.

*   *   *

Only a few hours ago Shona wouldn't have believed that she could forget about the loss of Toby because a bigger worry had imposed itself.

She left Mags and went in search of Jack. She found him in the garden, changed from his suit into old jeans and sweatshirt contemplating the rockery at the far side of the building.

'So you've seen fit to return?' he said when he saw her. 'So where were you?'

'There was a problem. I went to Crag Cottage and . . .'

'You are not in Langholme's employ as far as I'm aware?'

'Of course not.'

'Your work is here. The problems here are your concern. Or should be. If they are not then so be it. I have only this to say . . . your contract with me can be terminated at any time if that's what you want. Have I made myself clear? Now get yourself into the office. There's a list to be attended to at once.'

A REALISATION OF LOVE

In the office Shona busied herself with tidying Ingrid's desk and tried to thrust Jack's bitter words to the back of her mind. At least he could have allowed her to explain her actions and to tell him what she had discovered about Felix and Ingrid before condemning her.

She piled the loose papers on the desk into some sort of order so that anyone who took over from Ingrid would have a clear space to work on.

Expecting the drawers of the desk to be locked, she yanked so hard at the handle of the top one that she nearly fell backwards when it shot open.

Inside was the sort of paraphernalia she would expect: spare pens, envelopes, a box of staples and another of paper clips with some spilled out, a comb with a strand or two of Ingrid's red hair. The middle drawer contained more of the same together with an empty lunch box and a Thermos flask.

Beneath some paper in the bottom drawer Shona found Toby. She snatched him up with a cry of surprise. He had a label tied round his neck. She read it with rising horror.

'Look what I found, Felix,' it said. *'And you'll never guess where. Unless you and she are up to something on the quiet? You'd better have a good explanation. But I trust you, more fool me. So now your collection is complete again. Your loving Ingrid.'*

This was her Toby who had travelled with her from home whom she had grown to love and cherish. She turned him over and saw the slight nick at the bottom that was proof that he was hers.

'Oh Toby, I'm so sorry!' She clutched him to her in her relief that he was safe.

*   *   *

The door handle rattled and she pushed Toby beneath the papers on the desk to hide him from prying eyes.

Jack came in, changed now from his gardening clothes into his usual casual wear. She rose unsteadily to her feet.

'You left here and went to Crag Cottage to go off with someone for the day? Is that correct?' he said.

'I had to. There was a crisis. Or so I thought.'

'I see. And you went off knowing that Ingrid wasn't here to cope in your absence?'

The expression on Jack's face alarmed her.

She cleared her throat. 'There's something I have to tell you,' she said. 'I think I know where Ingrid has gone . . . who with, I mean.'

'You think you know?' Jack's voice was sharp.

She was almost afraid to continue. 'I'm certain.'

He walked across to the window and stood with his shoulders hunched. She had the feeling that he was oblivious of the wind now lashing the sycamores and the hint of rain on the glass.

The loaded silence lingered until she could bear it no longer. 'Felix and Ingrid have gone away together,' she said. 'They're an item. She's moving in with him and she's not coming back.'

He spun round. 'Ingrid and Felix Langholme? How do you know this?'

'His daughter told me.'

His initial disbelief turned swiftly to incredulity. 'That man and Ingrid?'

'I . . . I'm afraid so.'

She felt his intent gaze and turned her head away so that she wouldn't see his hurt. Ingrid had left him high and dry with no word of explanation. She hadn't told her parents either.

'I'm sorry,' Jack said, his voice tight.

'Ingrid won't want Tamsin anywhere near her,' she said after a short silence. 'I promised I'd look out for her. I have to do that. I can't

148

let her down.'

She clenched her trembling hands. Concern for the abandoned girl was like a lingering pain. She minded so much it hurt. And in order to look after her she knew she would have to leave Ferniehope Castle. Somewhere. Somehow. Perhaps Jodie would let them doss down in the apartment for a while until Felix could be contacted and arrangements made.

She took in a quivering breath that turned to a sob.

Ashamed, she turned and ran, needing to be on her own to deal with the shock of knowing the truth at last. She cared far more for Tamsin's welfare than she did for Felix.

$$*\qquad*\qquad*$$

Jack threw himself down on Ingrid's chair and sat with his elbows on the desk and his head in his hands. He hadn't expected this and neither had Shona from her obvious distress.

The man wasn't worth it. No man who could cause Shona such anguish was worth it, but her loss was deep and he had to respect it. He didn't doubt that her courage would get her through it in time, but he wished he had the wisdom to help her now.

He raised his head and moved his right arm so that the pile of paper on the desk was disturbed.

What was this? A toby jug hidden here?

Shona's missing toby jug! It seemed like it. He held it in his hand in wonder . . . a toby jug on Ingrid's desk. In growing amazement he read the label, recognising Ingrid's handwriting. Written proof of who had entered Shona's apartment and stolen this from her bedside table. Did Shona know about this?

Jack stood up, ripping off the label and stuffing it in the pocket of his jeans. Shona would see it now and as quickly as he could get it to her. At least she would have something that might well provide a degree of comfort.

*   *   *

Shona pushed open the conservatory door and entered a world where light and peace surrounded her. The scent from Jack's special orchid hung in the air and she sat down on the basket chair nearest to it and let the healing tears flow.

How she would continue to care for Tamsin she didn't yet know but there must be a way. Felix, influenced by Ingrid, had made it plain who came first in his life in which there was little room for a wayward daughter. The school fees would probably be paid. But what of Tamsin's wishes in the matter? Surely they must count for something when she had nothing else going for her in her life?

They would manage somehow, the two of them. They had to.

At last she wiped her eyes, knowing she couldn't have the luxury of being on her own for long. From here she could detect sounds of the returning minibus. She was not about to leave Jack to cope today with everything even though her decision to leave had already been agonised over and finally made.

*   *   *

'How long have we got before dinner?' one of the returning clients called across to Shona as she returned to the hall intending to retrieve Toby and take him up to her apartment.

'Mags will be serving it very soon,' she said.

There were one or two more enquiries from the returning history group and she made sure they knew where the drying room was if they wished to leave their damp outer clothing there.

Before she could move towards the office she saw Jack. At the same moment the front door bell rang.

'See who that is, will you, Shona?' he said brusquely.

She did as he asked, throwing open the door wide and surprised to see on the doorstep one of the old gentlemen she had met on her first evening here. His white hair had drops of moisture on it and the shoulders of his camel-haired jacket looked damp.

'Please come in,' she said cordially. 'Let me

take your coat.'

'Thank you, my dear. May I wish you good afternoon? But it's evening now, isn't it? Is that demanding employer of yours anywhere about?'

She smiled. 'He's just here, Mr Caruthers.'

Jack stepped forward. 'My dear Alfred,' he said warmly. 'This is an unexpected pleasure.'

'I was driving past and thought I'd drop in, see how you are getting on and if this young lady is doing her job well.'

'Very well,' said Jack smoothly. 'Will you stay and have dinner with us?'

The old man smiled. 'I'm so pleased you asked me. I accept with pleasure.'

'You're always welcome here, Alfred.'

'And afterwards perhaps I may be permitted to talk to your guests. History is my subject as you know, dear boy. I'm always hoping to learn something new.'

'I expect you'll be able to put them in the picture about historical sites locally,' said Jack. 'They should consider themselves lucky.'

Alfred Caruthers smiled at Shona. 'I'm the lucky one.'

'Inform Mags, will you?' said Jack, turning to her. 'And I think this is yours?' he added, holding Toby out to her.

She took Toby from him in silence knowing he would have read the missing label and was aware of the implications. But now, with a personal dinner guest and the evening's

152

entertainment to oversee, she was safe for the moment from any more grilling from Jack.

She escaped gladly to her apartment to hide Toby away before changing into something more presentable than her jeans and T-shirt.

*   *   *

Next morning she slipped out of the castle early. The sky looked uniform grey but the rain and wind of yesterday afternoon had gone leaving the garden bathed in chilly freshness.

Her sleep last night had been surprisingly deep and dream-free. Now she felt alert and ready for anything. Or almost anything. Sobered suddenly by the thought of what lay ahead, she walked slowly across the grass.

The area at the side of the building where Jack had been working on the new rockery looked well-tended with the flowerbed near the wall freshly dug and raked and looking as if it had taken hours of hard work to achieve. In reality Jack could only have been out here a short while because he had been in Carlisle for the day. Why had he attacked it so ferociously?

She thought of the first time she had seen him with the rake on his shoulder, looking relaxed as he greeted her. The sunshine had lightened his fair hair to gold and the expression on his tanned face had been friendly and interested. He had joked with her

153

about some of the courses on offer here at Ferniehope Castle. Gardening hadn't been mentioned though. Perhaps he thought of it as a normal way of life and not unusual enough to attract the people he hoped would come.

Ferniehope Castle was a beautiful setting in which to take time away from your real life, learning new skills or enjoying your special interests in the company of like-minded people.

Her real life was working here where the satisfaction of looking after the comfort of the guests was enormous.

What else had Jack said was on offer . . . canoeing, origami, cordon bleu cookery?

The courses sounded glamorous and it was bad luck that they had got Rex and his rambling club to start off the season, but the wildlife and history people were brilliant. Others would come no doubt, wanting to learn about navigation in arctic waters or potholing for the dumbfounded. A joke, of course. Jack had grinned when he saw her surprise and she had smiled back at him to show she wasn't fooled.

Jack didn't joke now. She had hardly seen him smile these last few days.

She bent down and picked up a small clump of earth that yesterday's raking had missed. It felt damp and sticky in her hand.

All at once she was shaken with compassion for him and his hopes and dreams. He was a good man, kind and caring. He deserved the success he worked so hard for. Why should the Felixes of this world charm their way effortlessly into everyone's affections when men like Jack were worth so much more?

'WHY DOES IT HAVE TO BE YOU?'

Shona's responsibilities to the history group were over for the time being once the minibus drove away. She stood on the doorstep to wave them off and then went into the office.

The group had planned visits to more archaeological sites today and wouldn't be back until late to make the most of a day that promised to be warm and drier than yesterday. Jack wasn't on the premises either because she had overheard him telling Mags to expect him back in time for lunch. So she had a free hour or two now to do what had to be done.

But before she could sit down at the computer her mobile rang. Jodie!

Her cousin was full of news of Duncan and the computer work he was getting. 'It's snowballing, Shona,' she said. 'He's even doing one-to-one tutorials now.'

'I'm so pleased for him,' said Shona. 'You too, Jodie. He'll be setting up his own business soon.'

'He's researching the help he can get and

grants and all that.'

Although Shona was thrilled at the news she had immediate things to think about too. She had to write the best resignation letter she could manage, explaining her reason for leaving Ferniehope Castle. She wanted to make the importance to her of the promise she had made to Tamsin quite clear to Jack so that he wouldn't think she had been unhappy here.

Of course she hadn't known at the time that her offer to look out for Tamsin would come to this. But it made no difference. She would be there for the girl as she had said even though it meant leaving Jack's employment where she had felt so much at home.

She leaned back in the chair and gazed at the yellow orchid on the high windowsill above the desk. The window faced north and that was ideal. She had learnt that much about orchids in her time here. It seemed happy enough there, its yellow flowers looked as if someone had formed them from wax. The dark green shiny leaves looked decidedly healthy.

She would take her morning coffee into the conservatory when she had written her letter and printed it out. There she could relax a little and feast her eyes on the array of exotic blooms. This might even be for the last time if Jack was successful in finding her successor swiftly.

A dull pain at the thought of this should be

squashed at once. Opening a new file on the computer, Shona stared at the blank screen that would soon be filled with words she didn't want to write.

She wondered what Tamsin was doing at the moment . . . hopefully making herself useful at Bessie's Kitchen. With luck Liz would be prepared to keep her for a few days until Jack could sort something out about a replacement and she could leave Ferniehope Castle with a clear conscience.

With a heavy heart Shona raised her hands above the keyboard and began to type.

Engrossed, she wasn't aware of Jack's return until she heard the front door slam. Startled she stayed quite still and waited to see what he would do.

She heard footsteps in the hall, his voice calling for Mags and the kitchen door closing. A few minutes only and then he was opening the office door.

She felt his presence like a blast of cold air. 'Shona?'

He towered over her as he read the words on screen. 'What's the meaning of this?' he asked.

She couldn't say anything for the lump in her throat. But she didn't have to because the words were there in front of him, clear in black on white.

The silence was like thunder as she waited for his reaction. 'So . . . what do you intend to do?'

'I'll think of something.' She wrenched a tissue from the box on the desk and scrubbed at her face. 'I had to decide quickly, Jack. Tamsin needs someone to look out for her. She'll never be happy with Ingrid who hates her. I can't bear the thought of her not being wanted, feeling pushed out.'

'But surely her father . . . '

'I don't know about Felix any more. I think he'll listen to Ingrid.'

'But why does it have to be you?'

'I promised. She trusts me. She's so lonely and unhappy.'

Again the long silence broken this time by the ringing of the telephone. With an exclamation of annoyance Jack picked up the receiver, perching on the corner of the desk to answer the call, 'Ferniehope Castle. Jack Cullen.'

His nearness was disturbing and Shona moved a little to be as far away from him as she could.

Suddenly he straightened and got to his feet, listening intently. 'Which ward? Cree? Thank you for telling us so promptly. We'll notify the family of course. No problem there, Mark.'

Shona felt cold. Liz . . . Tamsin?

Jack was listening again and then he spoke. 'Yes, we'll get something organised about getting them up here. And the rest of you will carry on as long as you feel able. We can lay on lunch here if that would help. It wouldn't? Afternoon tea then if you're back by then. Your decision.'

Shona let out the breath she was holding. Someone from the history group, obviously, perhaps badly injured. She looked up at Jack in concern.

For a moment after he put the phone down he stood with his hand on the receiver, deep in thought.

'Can I do anything to help?' she said at last.

With a start he seemed to remember she was there, still seated at the desk. 'There's been an accident,' he said.

'An accident . . . where? Who is it?'

One of the group collapsed apparently, went down like a ninepin. The girl, Deirdre. Not unconscious for long, luckily.'

'Where were they?'

'They'd stopped at a viewpoint and were getting out of the minibus to look at the view. The paramedics were quickly on the scene and now she's in the local hospital. A couple of her friends are with her.'

Seconds later Shona had the file for the history group up on screen. 'You'll need her details,' she said.

'The phone number,' Jack said. 'Good girl.'

She scribbled it down on the handy pad and tore off the sheet to give to him.

'You'll need that,' he said. 'There's

something I've got to do.'

'You want me to contact them?'

'There's not much to say at the moment. Give them the hospital number. They may want to come up.'

She noted down the ward name and the name of the girl's parents who lived in Leeds. Then she found the number of the hospital so they could phone them for reassurance.

By the time she had done that Jack had gone. She felt a moment's dismay. But there was much to do and no time to wonder more than briefly why he had left her to cope with the arrangements on her own.

$$*\qquad*\qquad*$$

The history group returned in the middle of the afternoon by which time the injured girl's parents were on their way to Ferniehope and due to arrive in about an hour. Mags had organised a room to be put at their disposal.

'It's on the ground floor, one we keep for our own guests,' she said.

'Sounds perfect,' said Shona rather distractedly. 'Is Jack home yet?'

'Not a sign of him,' said Mags disapprovingly.

'I'll phone the hospital now. They might be able to tell me if that's where he is.'

Shona asked if the girl's friends would like a lift back and found that they would. Calling her intention to Mags, she pulled on her jacket and went out to her car. It was the least she could do to collect them herself. Jack would have done the same, she felt sure, had he been here.

She found the two girls outside the main entrance of the hospital, clad in walking gear and looking anxious.

'Thanks,' one of them said as they clambered in. 'It was a shock Deirdre collapsing like that. She's never done anything like that before in her life.'

'They're keeping her in for tests,' the other one said, clicking on her seat belt.

'We'll get a coffee or something on the way back,' said Shona. 'You look as if you need something hot and strong.'

'We sure do. Thanks.'

Shona pulled in to a wayside café and was glad to see the colour returning to their cheeks as soon as they got the hot liquid down them. After that they became more talkative and they were back at Ferniehope Castle in what seemed a very short time.

'He's not back yet,' Mags told her as she went through the kitchen. 'Mr and Mrs Drew came but a minute or two ago. I put them in the lounge and gave them a cup of tea. The group leader, Mark, is putting them in the picture now.'

Shona felt exhausted by the time she had greeted Deirdre's parents and shown them to their room. Then she pointed out to them on the map how to reach the hospital and sent them on their way.

'So that's done,' she told Mags, sinking on to a kitchen stool.

It was only when she had drunk the cup of tea that Mags poured for her that she remembered Liz at Bessie's Kitchen and her promise to be in touch as soon as she could. Whatever would Liz think of her neglecting her like this?

She pulled out her mobile.

*   *   *

Dinner that evening was a sombre affair. Talk of the day's events and no one seemed in the mood for the planned entertainment programme afterwards. Mark, the young leader of the group, looking more careworn than usual, decided that they would merely try to relax rather than take part in a quiz.

Mr and Mrs Drew returned later, unable to tell them any more about their daughter than they already knew. Since they had already eaten they retired early to their room.

At a loose end Shona joined Mags in the kitchen and helped with the clearing up so that the older woman could get off early.

'You're not still worried about Jack, are you?' Mags said, as she wiped down the draining board.

'Jack?' said Shona, as if she hadn't noticed that he hadn't yet returned.

Mags gave her a knowing look. 'He'll be ringing up soon to say he's staying the night wherever he is. There!' She looked triumphant as the phone in the kitchen came to life.

'You answer it,' said Shona.

Mags did so. 'Yes, of course I will, Jack. We'll see you tomorrow then.'

'Where is he?' said Shona.

'He didn't say exactly and I didn't ask,' said Mags. 'Miles away anyway and not choosing to drive back tonight. But don't you worry yourself, lassie. He's booked into a hotel. He was checking that all is well here, that's all, that you're seeing to everything here and coping with that lot.'

Shona smiled, thankful to know that he was safe.

AN UNDENIABLE PASSION

Shona was up early next morning and had already made herself a coffee when Mags came bustling into the kitchen bringing with her an aura of chilly air.

'The kettle's hot,' Shona said. 'Tea, Mags, before you get going?'

'Make one for Donald, too, will you, Shona? He'll be here in a while.'

'Donald's starting work this early?'

'Just felt he should be around in case he's needed.'

'You haven't heard anything more?' Shona said in alarm.

'No, no, lassie. Stay there while I get started on breakfast.'

But Shona couldn't sit still. 'I'll lay the tables.'

She was glad to have something to do. When she had finished she ran up to her room and took Toby from the bottom of her wardrobe where she had hidden him from prying eyes.

'There's a much better place for you than hiding away in here,' she told him, giving him a kiss. Carrying him downstairs she headed for the conservatory. Jack's toby jugs up on their high shelf would be surprised to have another companion, but that was the right and proper place for Toby to be. He would like it there. Travelling about the countryside had never been his scene.

She reached for the stool and placed it in position so that she could climb on it to reach high enough to place him among his new friends. Then back on the floor again she stood looking up at him.

'You'll be happy up there, Toby,' she said. 'You can look down on Jack's beautiful orchids and know you're in the best place in the world.'

164

'Better than Leckie Shore?' said a young voice behind her.

Shona spun round. 'Tamsin!'

The girl was in her short skirt again today with her thin legs encased in black tights. Her bright T-shirt accentuated the blue of her eyes. She looked glowing. 'Pleased to see me, are you?'

Shona was still gaping. 'But Tamsin, what are you doing here?'

'I've come to stay if you'll have me.'

'Did Liz send you?'

'Not exactly. She wanted to phone you first but I wouldn't let her. I wanted to give you a surprise so she drove me.'

'A shock more like,' said Shona. She felt weak at the knees. Events were spinning out of control. 'Where's Liz now?'

'Talking to Mags in the kitchen.'

'I'd better go and see her.'

'And leave me here all alone with Jack's precious orchids? Oh, look up there, Shona, another toby jug. Isn't he yours?'

'Not any longer,' said Shona firmly. 'Toby's where he belongs now.'

'Like me,' said Tamsin, her eyes dancing.

Shona sank down on the stool. 'Oh Tamsin, I don't know what to do. I don't know what's happening.'

'But Jack does.'

Shona's head shot up. 'Jack?'

'He said to fetch you. He needs to talk to

you.'

'He's back then. Where is he?'

Tamsin shrugged. 'Somewhere. Come on. We'll find him.'

Still bemused Shona followed her. Jack was in the dining room looking out of the back window.

He turned as they came in, his face brightening. 'Here you are, Shona. Let's find somewhere quiet to talk on our own.' He glanced at his watch. 'This place will soon be a madhouse.'

'I'll look after things here,' said Tamsin. 'I can help Mags serve the breakfasts and everything. You can trust me.'

'I think I can,' said Jack.

'Then go.'

He turned to Shona. 'Shall we? My car's at the front.' Moments later they were driving away.

'Where are we going?' she asked as they passed Bessie's Kitchen.

'That place Tamsin told me you liked. Leckie Shore?'

Leckie Shore, she thought, opposite the island where the tide used to roll out as far as it would go as it never had for her since she had returned to Galloway.

'I'd like that,' she said faintly.

Jack drove in silence until they went bumping along the rough track to the shoreline.

166

'The tide's right out today,' she said in wonder.

'And there's the island,' said Jack as he parked and they got out.

The breeze felt fresh on Shona's face.

He looked anxious. 'Are you cold without a jacket?'

'Not a bit,' she said, intent of looking across at the island. The higher ground was silhouetted against the sky, and it seemed like a fairytale place at this time of the morning. 'Shall we walk across?' he asked.

The wet sand was soggy in places but Shona remembered from long ago that there was an almost invisible causeway that linked the island to the mainland that was firm underfoot.

'I phoned Ingrid's mobile,' Jack said as they set out. 'I was able to put on some pressure to find out exactly where they were and then set off at once. I found them easily enough. We had unfinished business, Felix Langholme and I. Ingrid too.'

'Where were they?'

'Not as far away as I expected. A place called Dumthorne. There's a good hotel there where I spent the night. We had a lot of talking to do and arrangements to make.'

'I see.'

'In the end he admitted that the ugly rumours he's been spreading weren't true and that his squandering his share of the proceeds of the sale of the castle had nothing to do with me.

'I'm glad,' Shona said simply.

They reached the shore of the island and stood looking back the way they had come. The sky over the distant mountains was brightening to azure as the clouds moved away.

'So how long are they staying at this place, Dumthorne?'

'For three weeks or so until their wedding.'

'They're getting married?'

Jack's gaze was intent as he turned to look at her. 'That's the way it is.'

'I hope they'll both be happy,' she said.

'You mean that?'

She nodded. 'But it doesn't help Tamsin.'

'And that upsets you more than anything?'

'More than anything connected with Felix.'

He let out a long breath. 'That's why I went after them.'

'You went for my sake?' she marvelled.

'We've agreed that in future Tamsin's home will be at Ferniehope Castle,' he said. 'Her father will support her financially, pay her school fees and so on. And every now and again the two of them will go off on their own for some quality time. If you can call it that.'

'Oh Jack,' she said faintly.

'Mags will get a letter from Ingrid very soon, I hope she'll understand what made her daughter do this. Donald too.'

'Mags is big-hearted. And she loves Ingrid.'

'And I love you, Shona,' Jack said, his voice deep. 'I can't do without you, my dearest love.'

She gazed at him in wonder, knowing she couldn't live without him either. 'Jack?'

At once she was in his arms. 'Dearest Shona, I love you for your concern about the girl,' he whispered, his breath warm on her cheek. 'Have you enough to spare for me too?'

She felt herself quiver in his arms. 'How can you doubt it?' she said, marvelling at the joy flooding through her.

'I love you, Shona,' he said, his voice stronger now. 'Will you marry me and be concerned about me forever?'

She gave a little giggle. 'And will you be concerned for Tamsin?'

'Mags will if I'm not,' he said. 'She likes someone to spoil. And Liz too down at Bessie's Kitchen maybe needing her help sometimes, so Tamsin knows she's needed as well as loved. That girl's not going to lack for anything.'

'And I won't lack for anything either,' Shona said. 'I love you truly, Jack.'

He held her so close she could hardly breathe. 'Shona,' he murmured, his voice vibrating a little.

His kiss was long and passionate and she felt herself melt into it until she felt she was drowning.

She pulled away at last. 'The tide'll soon be

on the turn,' she said breathlessly. 'The water rolls in fast.'

'Then come on, my love. Let's go.'

Together they walked back across the causeway.

'Shall we put a couple more stones for luck on the cairn of stones, my love?' he said when they reached the beach.

Shona smiled, knowing that all the good fortune in the world was already hers.